THE OTHER DAVID

THE OTHER DAVID

A Novel of Suspense by
CAROLYN COKER

DODD, MEAD & COMPANY
New York

FOR BEN AND BERNICE COLE

With special gratitude to Paul Gillette.
Thanks also to Stephanie Kegan,
Katina Simoniello and Rosalind Harrel;
and for technical advice, Cal Coker.

Published by Dodd, Mead & Company, Inc.
79 Madison Avenue, New York, N.Y. 10016
Distributed in Canada by
McClelland and Stewart Limited, Toronto
Manufactured in the United States of America
First Edition

Library of Congress Cataloging in Publication Data

Coker, Carolyn.
  The other David.

  I. Title.
PS3553.04367085   1984   813'.54   84-4152
ISBN 0-396-08390-0

Chapter 1

The early mornings of October are cold in the Umbrian hills. On the platform at the Perugia train station, Andrea Perkins pulled the loose-fitting collar of her sweater out from under her coat and up around her neck. She purposely stood with her back to the half-empty benches provided for the passengers, trying to ignore the two young men there who called to her in heavily accented English.

"Come sit with us, signorina! You will be much warmer over here." They were helping to keep themselves warm with a shared bottle of Chianti. They both wore the rubber-soled shoes of the *cellerari*, the men who work in wineries.

"We will see that you stay warm . . ." the second one began, but the rest of his words were drowned out by the eerie sound of the train's whistle that announced its approach a few seconds before the engine rounded the hill.

Andrea was glad to be going back to Florence. Her restoration of a fresco at the Palazzo del Municipio in Perugia was finished. The once magnificent Italian Renaissance building had originally been the villa of Lorenzo de' Medici, his hillside retreat. Now, and for the previous two centuries, it served as Perugia's city hall.

Andrea's services had been loaned to the city by the

Galleria dell'Accademia of Florence, where she was spending a year's apprenticeship as assistant curator, on leave from her teaching position at Harvard's School of Fine Arts.

Things were the same all over Italy. Andrea had been stunned by the beauty of the priceless art in churches, hotels, municipal buildings, parks—wherever she turned. And she had been distressed by the condition of much of it.

"*Ciao, bambina.*" One of her admirers threw her a noisy kiss and headed, she was pleased to see, for the second-class car. The only passengers that joined her in first class were a disheveled-looking couple with three small children, and an old priest wearing a long white robe and carrying a bulky paper-wrapped package. The priest smiled at Andrea and insisted that she enter the train ahead of him.

Soon, the train lurched forward and slowly accelerated to an even pace. The few lights of the city slid past the window. Now there was only darkness that silvered the window and reflected her own face—and those of the two young men from the platform who stood behind her in the doorway.

"*Here* you are . . . and all alone. How sad," one of them said, slurring his words and swaying in the corridor more than was necessary to accommodate the movement of the train.

"Some vino?" The second one held the almost empty bottle out to her, managing to slosh a few drops on the carpet of the compartment.

"No, *grazie*," Andrea said, trying to be stern, but smiling at their condition in spite of herself as she closed the door in their faces and locked it. She heard their laughter outside and the scolding voice of the conductor telling them to get back to their own seats.

When it was quiet again, Andrea slipped off her coat and straightened the neck of her sweater. It was too large and drooped at the shoulders, but it was loose and comfortable and she loved it. It had been a gift from her sister, Joy.

Joy, with the lovely pale skin and wistful blue eyes—brave blue eyes that had given Andrea permission to roller skate and run and dance while her sister watched from a wheelchair. Joy, whose name was as ill-fitting as the sweater she had knitted for Andrea.

Andrea pulled down the curtain and leaned her head against the window. The rhythmic motion of the train lulled her into a light sleep that was undisturbed until the porter knocked on the door and announced *Firenze—Stazione Centrale*.

It was still early; that time between night and morning when the streetlights have gone off and the store lights have not yet come on. There was very little traffic except for the yellow Fiat taxis that zipped in and out of the passenger-loading area. The Accademia was only a few blocks away. Andrea decided to walk.

Fog swirled up from the Arno River and drifted across Florence, smoothing the sharp outlines of objects to an obscure blur.

The darkened street was quiet. The loudest sound was the clicking of Andrea's own high heels on the sidewalk. But soon there was another, softer sound; something behind her keeping a steady pace. She felt a prickling at the back of her neck when she realized she was being followed.

That in itself was not unusual; since the first day she arrived in Florence, whenever she walked along the street alone there was usually the sound of metal heel taps behind her. Following a beautiful woman was a favorite pastime of Italian men. And Andrea, with her long copper-colored hair and olive-green eyes, always drew attention.

But this time there was something different. It was not the familiar staccato footsteps hurrying to catch up with her—but a soft, shuffling sound. Was it the rubber-soled shoes of the winery workers who had tried to come into her compartment on the train?

She began to walk faster.

The sheer walls of the Galleria dell'Accademia loomed up through the fog like a fourteenth century fortress.

Andrea usually entered the museum by the massive front door, but decided now to go through the basement. It was closer. She turned into the narrow brick alleyway, almost running the last few yards to the heavy metal door. Her fingers were shaking as she unlocked and slammed it behind her.

"Luca!" She called the guard whose office was in the basement. There was no answer.

"Luca!"

He's asleep, she thought angrily. More than once he had staggered up from the chair by the front door where he napped, rubbing his eyes, waiting for the sound of her key in the lock to wake him.

Once through the door, Andrea slammed it, threw the dead bolt and hooked the chain lock, then leaned against the wall for a moment, holding her breath, but heard no sound from outside. Quietly crossing to the window next to the door, she pulled back the drawn blind a fraction of an inch and peered out through the steel grate just as her pursuer knocked.

She felt relieved—and at the same time foolish. Standing on the step holding a large brown-paper-wrapped package was a diminutive old priest in a long white robe and leather sandals, the same one she had seen on the train.

Andrea turned on the overhead light and unbolted the door. "Good morning, Padre. May I help you?"

4

"I frightened you, signorina?" He wore the faintest of smiles.

"No. Well, yes. I suppose just a little."

"How could either of us know our destination was the same?"

"With the fog . . . I couldn't see . . . Please come in."

"Of course, of course. It is only natural. Our rude young men must be a problem for you." He spoke in one of the many local dialects, and while Andrea spoke Italian very well, she had trouble with some of the Tuscany and Umbria hill-country accents. She doubted that even the natives understood them all.

"How can I help you, Padre?"

"Do you work here, signorina?"

"Yes. I am the assistant to the curator, Signore Vittorio Sassetti."

"It is my good fortune. I was afraid only a guard would be here at this hour and I was hesitant to leave this . . ." He looked down at the package in his arms. "This belongs in the Galleria."

"Let me take that. It must be heavy." Noticing for the first time how frail the old priest looked, Andrea took the package from him and placed it on a long metal table. "Won't you sit down?" She motioned to the only chair in the room that was not filled with books or canvases or picture frames.

"*Grazie. Molte grazie.*" His voice was as dry and brittle as a winter leaf. "I have just returned from the funeral of my sister," he said and crossed himself. Andrea inclined her head in sympathy. "She was old . . . It was time for God to call her," he continued without sorrow.

Then the priest began, haltingly, to tell Andrea about his family. Much of what he said she could not follow mainly because of his accent and his penchant for slipping into dialect. But she was able to piece together that his

5

father and grandfather had been farmers in the Tuscan hills. The priest and his sister, Maria, had been the last survivors. Andrea sat on the edge of the table listening politely and wondering why he was telling her all this.

"The small sum of money that was left after Maria's illness," the priest continued, "will be distributed by the church. But this . . ." he leaned forward and touched the package with a thin, gnarled finger, "this should be here at the Galleria dell'Accademia. It should be with the other one."

"The other one?" Andrea was not sure she had understood and waited for an explanation, but the priest merely nodded.

From the shape of the package she knew that it probably contained a painting. "Perhaps you should keep it for yourself, Padre. It must have meant a great deal to your family," Andrea said sincerely, but she was also thinking of the cabinets that lined the workroom filled with similar donations which had little value except to the donor.

"No, no," the priest quickly insisted, "it should be with the other one." He rose unsteadily, standing still a moment to get his breath.

"*Grazie*, Padre," Andrea almost sighed as she accepted it. "The Accademia will be grateful."

The priest patted her hand. His touch was like the flutter of a bird's wing against her skin. Then his voice grew louder and the words tumbled faster as he spoke of the tragic loss of so much of Italy's religious art. Andrea's translation of the rest of what he said was, "The church had almost waited too late to restore Leonardo's *Last Supper*." That was part of it. And there was something about Buonarroti . . . Giotto . . . Michelangelo . . . Leonardo . . . and once more, Buonarroti.

"I had not seen the portrait myself until yesterday." He straightened the long strand of wooden beads around his neck and clasped the heavy cross that hung near his waist. "Peasant superstition . . . stories four, five hundred years old, stories my mother heard from *her* mother as a child. 'It is best left locked away,' she told us. At the time my mother died, when I might have opened the trunk where the painting was stored if I had been curious, I had been in the Holy Order of San Miniato for several years and had little contact with the world outside the monastery walls. The picture was forgotten until yesterday," he said, and pulled feebly at the heavy basement door.

Andrea swung it open for him.

"*Grazie*, signorina." The priest crossed himself again and touched Andrea's forehead with one finger. "God's blessings."

Andrea stood in the open doorway and watched the priest until he reached the corner. His shoulders were straighter now and he walked almost jauntily—as though he had been relieved of more than the weight of the package.

Chapter 2

Andrea picked up the bulky package, weighing it in both hands a moment before reaching into the drawer for scissors to snip the knotted cord. She shook the paper away and placed the picture face up on the table.

Through the centuries of grime she could barely make out that it was a portrait of a young man. The priest's long-departed relative, she wondered?

The canvas was in good condition, but it would take hours to clean it properly, and there were any number of unfinished projects that had priority.

Then, running her fingers across the face of the canvas she felt a peculiar series of perforations in the upper-left-hand corner. Puzzled, she slowly followed the uneven pattern again, using only the tip of her forefinger this time.

Believing that a qualified restorer of paintings needed equal parts of skill and skepticism, she did not allow her thoughts to leap ahead and assume that the tiny holes were arranged in the pattern that immediately came to mind. But she impatiently shuffled the contents of the drawer until she found a battery-operated magnifying glass and focused on an area about two inches in diameter.

She could just make out a circular pattern. The design resembled an official seal she and every other professional in her field had seen many times—though usually only under protective glass on museum walls or illustrated in textbooks.

If the medallion were authentic, it would provide the opportunity anyone in her profession hoped to have, if only once in a lifetime. But she knew how unlikely such a discovery would be. As a restorer and authenticator of paintings, her scientific testing had unmasked many an artful forgery and discovered mere mistakes. She had learned to make no assumption, no judgment, no emotional response until the facts were in.

Keeping all this in mind, she picked up the painting and started up the stairs to her office. Any previous plans she had made for the morning would have to wait until she examined the medallion.

As she entered the great hall she was greeted by the musty smell of the huge Flemish tapestries that hung on the two long walls. They were a backdrop for six of the Accademia's eight famous statues by Michelangelo. Andrea hardly glanced at them. Instead, she looked straight ahead to the specially built apse at the end of the hall where the magnificent statue of David stood. Seeing Michelangelo's *David* each morning was still one of the greatest compensations of her job.

Later, when the museum was open to the public, swarms of tourists with their cameras would stare at the statue of the young warrior who stood poised, in a moment of expectation, his left knee slightly bent, ready to run into combat. They would photograph him and each other. But for a few minutes each morning, David belonged to her.

. . . *he was ruddy, and withal of beautiful countenance, and goodly to look to.*

With only those words of description from the first Book of Samuel in the Old Testament, Michelangelo had conceived this masterwork.

Yes, goodly to look to, Andrea thought as she always did when she saw the statue. Simple words, but she could think of no better way to describe the shepherd boy who became king.

The beauty of the statue had had the same profound effect on her as a sudden infatuation—a new love. She had wanted to know everything about David the man.

Andrea was hardly a biblical scholar. She had drifted away from her Methodist Sunday school in her early teens. Certainly she had never read the Bible for pleasure. But once she began, she found Samuel's account of David's life fascinating. She read and reread it until the florid language seemed natural and she could visualize the action—feel the writer's passion.

Let David, I pray thee, stand before me; for he has found favor in my sight . . .

To Andrea he was a frozen moment of male perfection she had never come close to finding in human form. Perhaps because the analytical Andrea was given too loose a rein. She was allowed to stand coolly in the shadows taking notes on every nuance of a relationship—weighing strengths and weaknesses as though they could be converted to metric measurements. With only one man had she lost all sense of detachment and he, as it happened, was as unattainable as the graceful marble statue.

The quiet of the Accademia was shattered by a rasping snore from the sleeping guard by the front door. Andrea went into her office.

There were framed and unframed pictures, large and small propped against all four walls of the tiny room. Behind her desk was a crude wooden table crowded with a random assortment of bottles and jars of oils and chemicals, and a large chunk of beeswax next to her travel iron. She used the iron and wax for repairing torn canvases.

Andrea had started college intent on becoming a

painter. But by her sophomore year she realized that while she had above-average talent, she would never be great. And that was what she wanted to be. To her surprise, however, she discovered that she had extraordinary ability at restoration and a bent for art history. She gave up painting and was content—and in demand—to restore the masterpieces painted by others.

Reaching in her desk drawer, she took out a glass beaker, then dug around in the jumble of the table until she found the ingredients she needed. Mixing together five parts of absolute alcohol, three parts of turpentine, and one part of ethyl acetate, she stirred the mixture with a glass rod and poured a small amount into a shallow dish. Next to the dish she lined up a box of cotton balls and a bottle of castor oil.

She dipped a cotton ball in the solvent and began at the top left-hand corner, rubbing the canvas in small circles, frequently replacing a soiled cotton ball with a new one.

Soon, enough of the medallion was uncovered to reveal exactly what she had imagined was there—a sword and a swan in the arches of an *M* encircled by a garland of flowers.

Refusing to give in to a simmering feeling of excitement, Andrea reached for *The Illustrated Encyclopedia of Renaissance Art* that leaned permanently against her desk. She flipped through a few pages and found an exact duplicate of the design on the picture. There was a notation which read: ". . . in 1482 Lorenzo de' Medici (Il Magnifico) devised the above medallion to identify literature, music, philosophical papers, paintings, poetry, and other contributions from the scores of creative thinkers to whom he was patron. Among the towering artists of the day were Verrocchio, Michelangelo, Filippino Lippi, and Ghirlandaio."

So, Andrea thought, it was indeed the Medici Medallion.

Yet there was no guarantee that it was authentic.

She poured more solvent into the dish and continued the laborious task of cleaning the canvas. She prided herself on being able to tell when she had reached the minuscule layer of varnish that was painted over the actual pigment of the oil-based paint as protection. But she constantly checked the cotton for a trace of color. If there had been the slightest coloration she would have used the castor oil as a sort of fire extinguisher to stop the "burning in."

A brilliant blue background was emerging.

Andrea was so engrossed in the mechanics of what she was doing that it was at least thirty minutes before the realization of what lay beneath the centuries of grime struck her.

When she knew, she stopped and stared, unbelieving, at the picture. Then, calling up the same kind of self-control it would take to dismantle a ticking bomb, she forced her hand to be steady and continued. Now she knew what the priest meant—that it should be with the other one.

The basement door banged shut. Vittorio Sassetti and his wife, Rosa, had arrived. A few minutes later, Rosa waved through the office doorway to Andrea and "*Buon giorno, cara*. Welcome back!" trailed after her as the woman rushed into the reception room to answer the phone. Andrea had not noticed that it was ringing.

The face in the portrait had the same youthful beauty, courage, and determination as the statue. But the eyes were vivid blue, the hair that curled around the face was deep, gleaming bronze—and the warm flesh tones of the strong neck and face gave pulsating life even beyond the dimension of the white Carrara marble.

There it was. The same face she admired each morning. It was a portrait of David.

Andrea still did not allow herself to believe that it was

more than a copy painted by one of the master's students.

Working now from right to left, a signature was becoming visible. She could read Buonarroti. Of course, the priest had told her what the portrait was, but she had not understood. He had said Buonarroti.

When she began, she had been interested only in identifying the Medici Medallion. But now she was surprised that she had not felt what the portrait was, even through the coarse brown paper. The analytical Andrea was temporarily nowhere to be found.

She dropped the last cotton ball into the wastebasket. Her lips moved but no sound came out as she read the entire signature on the portrait of David to herself—*Michelangelo Buonarroti*.

Chapter 3

One could picture Vittorio Sassetti, the curator of the Accademia, grandly taking the podium at La Scala and quieting the crowd with the lift of a single finger. He had that kind of presence. And when it was an audience of one, as now, he could be formidable.

"Sleeping! *Dio mio!* Is that what you are paid to do . . . to let the world break into the basement?" Vittorio loomed over Luca, the guard, who, until that moment, had indeed been asleep at the front door.

Luca blinked up at Vittorio and hurriedly stood at attention. "I sat down for just an instant, only a few moments ago," Luca sputtered, glancing nervously from Vittorio to Rosa Sassetti, who smiled sympathetically but did not intervene with her husband. Luca was a tall, slender young man with hair and eyes the color of walnut stain. He was a former student of the Accademia and the son of one of the patrons. If his ambition had matched his talent, he could have made a living selling pictures in the Straw Market.

"Only a few moments ago, eh? Then why is there no notation of a two A.M. check on the security board?" Vittorio used his hands like an orchestra conductor when he was angry. For this performance his baton was a rolled-up copy of *Signore*, an explicit sex pictorial he had found in the basement security office. Arms outstretched for the overture, he began, "I do not wonder that your father is concerned about you." Softly now, fingers cupped together in an upward motion, cuing in the strings—"You have talent, you could be an artist." Bringing in the percussion—"But, no! You were more interested in getting the models into bed than painting them!" Full ensemble now—"Go downstairs and check all the cabinets and clean up your office. And I don't want to see any more of these . . ." he said, hurling the copy of *Signore* at Luca's feet, "these . . . *magazines* lying around down there."

Andrea, who was standing in the doorway of her office as Vittorio turned away from the stricken Luca, said, "Vittorio, could you come in here for a moment?"

"Ah, *cara*!" Vittorio whirled toward her and gave her a hug, his anger dissipated, its energy converted to ebullience.

Andrea told him sketchily of her meeting with the priest, then handed the portrait to Vittorio.

He walked to the window, holding the picture up in the bright sunlight, examining it at arm's length, then a few inches from his face—both the front of the canvas and the back. Finally he put the painting down on Andrea's desk. "Where did you get this?"

Somewhat surprised by his intent expression, Andrea explained again in more detail. "It was probably painted right here at the Accademia. A student with a bit of larceny in his heart signed Michelangelo's signature and made himself a fistful of lire. There's no question that it's old . . . maybe several centuries. But I've come to believe that art forgery is the second oldest profession." She smiled at what she thought would be a shared joke, but the curator's expression did not change.

Andrea had great respect for Vittorio. She found his textbook knowledge of art a little lacking in some areas,

15

but he had learned about art by growing up in this magnificent city that was one huge Renaissance museum. He had grown to know and love the architecture, statuary, fountains, and monuments he confronted on almost every street corner. But surely, Andrea thought, he had not come to believe the stories passed down through the centuries of fabled works of art by da Vinci, Giotto, Michelangelo, and other artistic giants; stories that concerned paintings, superior to any now known, that had been hidden away. Some purported masterpieces had actually surfaced—all had proved to be fakes.

"*L'altro*," Vittorio said softly. The other one.

"But surely you don't believe . . ." Andrea began.

"No. No, no," Vittorio said expansively, throwing out his hands. "It is just that all my life I have heard stories of 'the other one' . . . the portrait of David that Michelangelo is said to have painted as a gift for his patron, Lorenzo de' Medici. How wonderful it would be to discover such a painting, yes, *cara*?" Vittorio laughed and patted Andrea's shoulder.

"Of course . . ."

"I know, I know—impossible," Vittorio said with a self-deprecating shrug.

"I'd say highly unlikely." Andrea did not make positive statements without proof, and there was a staggering amount of evidence that the painting was a fake. The first and most convincing fact for Andrea was that Michelangelo was a sculptor, not a painter. The Sistine Chapel, yes, but that was frescoes. Michelangelo painted frescoes. "He didn't paint easel paintings," she said to Vittorio, who had picked up the canvas and was studying it again.

"You are right, of course, but there is the Doni tondo."

"*One* easel painting, then. Only one in his whole body of work."

Michelangelo had been commissioned by Agnolo Doni to paint an easel portrait of the Madonna as a wedding gift for Doni's bride. The painting now hung in the Uffizi Gallery in Florence.

"But we must put David under the microscope because of the age of the canvas, at least," Vittorio said a little wistfully, wanting to believe they had found *L'altro* but knowing that the microscope and X ray were not kind to dreams.

Andrea had intended to test it thoroughly, at any rate. Her profession demanded that kind of thoroughness, though she remained a skeptic. But any painting over one hundred years old deserved to be identified, if possible.

She reached for a large piece of cardboard on the floor behind her desk. Mounted on it was a photograph of a small fraction of Michelangelo's "Creation of Adam" from the ceiling of the Sistine Chapel. It showed only the upper quarter of the left side of Adam's face. In this enlargement, the artist's brush strokes were discernible. Brush strokes—the way an artist laid on paint—were like fingerprints to Andrea.

She placed the photograph next to the portrait and swung the eyepiece of the twenty-power long-arm binocular-microscope in front of Vittorio. He looked first at the enlargement, then through the microscope. "They look the same to me," he said.

Andrea adjusted the focus and looked through the eyepiece. The smooth thin brush strokes in the portrait seemed identical to those in the photograph.

"And notice the crackle," Vittorio said.

The notation of crackle was one of the first steps in dating a painting. All old pigment ultimately developed a network of fine hairlike cracks. But clever forgers could create it by running a sharp instrument over the surface of a painting and rubbing dirt into the cracks to make it look old. Some didn't even bother to do this, but painted the crackle on with a single-hair paintbrush. Andrea, however, had never doubted the age of the painting. The priest had told her it had been in his family for hundreds of years.

"And something else . . ." Vittorio said, disappearing through the doorway just as Andrea looked up. In a moment he returned with a large book—a copy of Condivi's biography of Michelangelo. He leafed through until he found the page he was looking for. "Here." He pointed to the last two items in a long list of works by the artist. They were:

Easel Painting #1
Easel Painting #2

It was not hard for Andrea to understand why they had been listed in this manner without so much as a title. Condivi had written his biography at the artist's request and with his collaboration near the end of Michelangelo's life. It was made clear in the biography that the artist held painting and painters in contempt. There had long been a controversy concerning the respective merits of painting and sculpture. This became a burning issue in Michelangelo's lifetime, and he saw himself as the leader of the sculptors. Painting, he stated, was good to the extent that it resembled sculpture and sculpture was bad to the extent that it resembled painting.

"One of the two easel paintings was the Doni tondo," Vittorio said, "but the second has never been identified."

"You know there are inaccuracies in this biography . . ."

"Of course, of course." Vittorio threw his hands out in a gesture of total agreement. "Interesting, though . . ."

"Yes, it is interesting." Andrea smiled at Vittorio's attempt at objectivity. "Shall we take it into X-ray?"

18

The lab was equipped for chemical testing, but Andrea avoided using chemicals. Some of them were hard to control and could damage a piece of art. She preferred using X-ray, ultraviolet, or a carbon-14 test.

Vittorio sat in the only chair in the clinical-looking room. He shrugged and took the pose of a moderately interested observer.

First she situated the portrait on a long metal table, switched off the overhead lights and turned on the ultraviolet light in the large windowless room. The picture fluoresced uniformly. If there had been bright spots, if part of the canvas had glowed with more intensity than the rest, it would have indicated retouching—or painting over the original.

Next she took a small scalpel-like instrument and removed a sliver of wood the size of a toothpick from the frame and dropped it into a metal dish. She burned the wood in a scintillation counter to measure the amount of carbon present. The count would indicate when the tree from which the frame had been made had stopped living. Later, when she calculated the results, she discovered the frame was only two hundred years old. To be authentic, the portrait would have to be nearly five hundred.

Vittorio looked crestfallen. But Andrea almost reluctantly pointed out that the age of the frame alone did not discredit the painting. She showed him what she had discovered earlier—that the canvas had been cut from its original frame at some time (according to the carbon-14 test, two hundred years ago) and attached to a newer, stronger frame. She pointed out the yellow smudges of glue around the outer edges of the wood.

X-ray would reveal much more than the first two tests.

"If it was a gift to Lorenzo de' Medici . . ." Vittorio, speaking mainly to himself, was trying to construct a history for the portrait, "it must have been in the Medici

Palace here in Florence during the Savonarola purge . . ."

"Of course!" Andrea said almost triumphantly, her mind racing, computing facts and dates she had taught her art history classes at Harvard. "And you're forgetting something." This was a period of art history she knew very well. In fact, she had written an article for *U.S. Art Review* about the Medici family, who had fostered the art and literature that ushered in the Renaissance. In a follow-up article she had contrasted them with the destructive influence of the self-styled religious zealot, Savonarola, in the same era.

"What do you mean?" Vittorio asked.

"The fire! If the portrait had been in the palace when Savonarola and his followers arrived, it would have been burned."

"Not necessarily."

Grudgingly she admitted to herself that he was right. True, Savonarola had led a mob to the palace, instructing them to burn or destroy everything inside as a protest against what he termed Florence's "ostentation and self-indulgence." Piero de' Medici, who had taken over the leadership of the city after the death of Lorenzo two years earlier, fled to Venice with his family and escaped only hours before the fire. But everything had not been destroyed. Over the years, commemorative coins that were known to have been in the palace had turned up, along with several manuscripts.

"It is mere speculation," Vittorio began tentatively, "but suppose an ancestor of the priest's was a part of the mob. He might have decided to keep the portrait for himself."

"It is possible that it was painted by a contemporary of Michelangelo's . . ." Andrea busied herself with the master panel of dials and switches beneath the tiny leaded glass window that looked back into the X-ray room at the portrait. "It might have been a student . . . or a protégé."

During the next several minutes the X-ray camera scanned the entire surface of the painting. Several times Andrea stopped to photograph, first one of the eyes, then a section of cheek, a portion of hair. These pictures would indicate how the painter had built up the underpainting. Andrea cautioned herself when she realized that instead of "the painter" she was thinking "Michelangelo." She could tell visually it was the method he had used, and she knew that there were supporting charts and descriptions of his technique that corresponded to the X-ray photographs.

When they had completed the testing, the information they had would ordinarily be enough to establish the age and authenticity of a painting.

And, there was the Medici Medallion. The perforated design in the corner of the painting had proved to be an exact duplicate of the official emblem used by the Medici to identify favored manuscripts and paintings. But that could be faked, too. It could have been done with the point of a pin. Andrea would not allow herself to believe it was genuine without absolute proof.

"We'll have to have someone else examine it, too," Vittorio said, speaking her thoughts.

"Yes." Then they were both silent, not knowing how to proceed with something of this potential magnitude.

"We should not mention it to anyone outside just yet," Vittorio said.

"No."

"Or announce it. I mean, to La Nazione . . . or television . . ."

"Oh, no!" Andrea had not even thought of the press, the international attention the portrait would generate.

"Maybe I should call the Uffizi and have someone stop by tomorrow."

"Their equipment is no better than ours—not as good.

No," Andrea said, "we should call Houston, Texas—the Clint J. McCauley Museum."

Andrea was surprised at the difficulty she still had saying McCauley's name after almost a year. She was even more surprised—no, dismayed, by the slight quickening of her pulse.

Chapter 4

The McCauley Museum in Houston, Texas, was comparatively new, built shortly after World War II. It had begun on a grand scale and continued to grow so that now the museum was considered to have a collection of Renaissance art second only to that of the Metropolitan in New York. Most of the inventory had come directly from the private collection of its benefactor, Clint J. McCauley, with additions purchased from private collectors, none of whom were well known in art circles. Jealous directors of longer established Eastern institutions sniffed and whispered that most of the "private collectors" were GIs who had found themselves in Italy during the war. It was rumored that a small group of artillerymen had confiscated a number of valuable paintings from Italian homes and smuggled them into the United States rolled in wax paper inside their weapons. None of this had been proved, and the story was first heard from a disgruntled former employee of the McCauley. So, in Texas at least, it was not given much credence.

Consulting the McCauley Museum, it seemed to Andrea, was the obvious next step in testing the portrait of David. Not because of the expertise of its curator, Tom Daley, but because of the museum's equipment.

Andrea had worked with Daley at a privately endowed

museum near the campus when she was at Harvard before he had been offered the position in Houston. She had always considered him a pedantic caretaker rather than a creative curator. However, he now had dominion over the McCauley's X-ray nondispersive analyzer. This remarkable microcomputer could prove without question the age and composition of paint and canvas. It could even measure the amount of pressure applied to a paintbrush by an artist in signing his signature—and compare it to a known original. So far, the McCauley Museum had the only computer with this type of sophistication, and the results of its examinations were accepted internationally as conclusive.

Andrea was well acquainted with the scope of information available from the Mc36 computer because she had helped to program it at Clint McCauley's request.

She had met McCauley through an assignment for the Newman Gallery in New York. The owner, Wilkie Newman, hired her occasionally to help with examining and repairing paintings acquired in large estate sales. So she had not been surprised to receive a call from him one winter afternoon; but instead of offering her a project as she expected, he had invited her to join him and Clint McCauley for lunch the following week at the Plaza Hotel.

February still stalked Fifth Avenue and 59th Street when she arrived in New York, but spring was blooming inside the Oak Room of the Plaza. Sun-yellow jonquils and scarlet tulips sat in white china vases on white tablecloths at every table. The flowers were a sharp contrast to the dark, almost black, heavy oak paneling and Corinthian columns in the high-ceilinged room.

Andrea spotted Newman near the back and began weaving her way through the luncheon crowd in his direction.

Shortly after she was seated Newman looked toward the entrance and said, "Ah, here he is." Andrea watched

McCauley's progress across the room. He had taken only a few steps when he was stopped by an Arab gentleman in a flowing white robe who left his own party to speak with the Texan. The Arab's full lips moved quickly and with much animation, then he smiled and bowed, backing away. McCauley nodded and started toward the back of the room again. He stopped and spoke to a lovely white-haired actress for whom a Broadway theater had just been named. She took his hand in both of hers and said something that made him chuckle. There were other men and women in the room who seemed to be watching McCauley expectantly, hoping to be recognized, but now he came straight to the table where Andrea and Newman were seated.

Newman made the introductions. McCauley took Andrea's hand. She looked up into the face of a man in his early fifties. His hair was sun-bleached, and his blue eyes were clear and probing. The few wrinkles around his mouth and eyes were squint lines against the Texas sun and contrasted with the tan of the rest of his face. His beige wool suit was expertly tailored to his tall, lean frame, and his shoes were the kind that are handcrafted in Italy. But the overall impression was of a man as comfortable in dungarees on his ranch as he obviously was in the posh Oak Room of the Plaza Hotel.

"Miss Perkins, I just bought one of your paintings from the Newman Gallery," McCauley said, pulling a chair out from the table.

"Oh, no. I'm not a painter," Andrea said, wondering if she was here under false pretenses, "I restore paintings."

"The Arnoldi," Newman said. "He bought the Arnoldi *Portrait of a Young Girl* that was in such abysmal condition." Wilkie Newman had the annoying habit of acting as an interpreter, racing ahead in conversations, contributing little of his own, but repeating or anticipating the responses of others. McCauley ignored him.

"I saw the portrait last month," McCauley said, "but decided it was beyond repair. What you were able to do with that painting was as much a work of art as Arnoldi's original concept. You should have added your own signature."

Score one for the graceful compliment, Andrea thought.

During lunch McCauley explained the reason he had been anxious to talk with her. He had given an endowment to MIT to develop a computer to work in conjunction with an X-ray machine for determining the authenticity of art objects. His own knowledge of computers and his interest in art had convinced him that such a machine could be invaluable for his museum. He had arranged with two full professors who occasionally did consultant work for McCauley Computers to develop it. The Mc36 was nearly completed, he told her, "but those scientific types need someone with your expertise to help program it."

Andrea assured him that she had neither the experience nor the inclination to program computers. But by the time they had finished lunch she had agreed to at least meet with the MIT scientists. As she left, buttoning her coat against the blast of cold air that attacked her on Fifth Avenue, she was actually looking forward to the computer project—or more accurately, to its completion, when McCauley would be back to see it demonstrated.

The next two months Andrea spent many hours with the two avuncular scientists who had developed the Mc36. She learned to operate it, and, to her surprise, was able to contribute crucial information they had not realized was important. For instance, the first determination the computer made in examining an oil painting was the age of the varnish, the protective final layer of paint. Andrea suggested that if the varnish proved to be of fairly modern vintage, the notation be made: *Inconclusive—analyze pigment*. It was not uncommon to add additional coats of varnish years after a painting was completed as protection, so it could easily postdate the original, but pigment could be dated absolutely. The same caution to continue testing applied to glue—even if it turned out it came from an Elmer's tube. Canvases were often stripped from their original frames and affixed to newer, sturdier ones. Another of her contributions was to assist the original programmer in compiling a list of the composition of various pigments. They ranged from lampblack (black, strictly speaking, is not a pigment, but always some form of soot from organic matter) to ultramarine, made from powdered lapis lazuli, to carmine red, made by grinding dried cochineal insects.

Proud of her contribution to the project, Andrea was pleased to be asked to demonstrate the Mc36 at its debut at the Boston Museum of Fine Arts.

A layer of snow still clung to the granite of the Boston Museum, softening it, making it less imposing when she arrived. In the parking lot in the rear there was the usual collection of compact cars, some of them with clumps of ice still clinging to their tops and in crevices of the fenders. But next to the door leading into the basement stood a clean, dry Rolls-Royce the same noncolor as the snow, but with a higher gloss. McCauley must already be here, Andrea thought, and began to walk faster.

Inside the basement room a folding metal table had been set up, and on it sat the typewriter-sized microcomputer with its two-by-three-inch television screen. A jumble of connecting cables ran under the table and connected to a portable X-ray machine. The picture Andrea had chosen to use for the demonstration was already on the rack in the X-ray viewing room. It was a portrait of a dandyish gentleman with a pointed beard and large mustache. He wore a red velvet cap rakishly on the side of his head. The portrait was purported to have been painted by Van Dyck.

She was about to ask her MIT associates where everyone was when a dozen or so people came down the stairs from the first floor. They had apparently been viewing the museum's new exhibition of Egyptian art. Andrea spotted McCauley instantly and he came directly to greet her. He took her hand and the white squint lines on his face disappeared in a smile. She was surprised to feel a strange little thump in her chest like a lightly tossed bean-bag at the pleasure of seeing him again.

McCauley left her and went to sit in one of the folding chairs. This seemed to be a signal for the others (the people from the Boston Museum, Wilkie Newman, Tom Daley, and two of his assistants from McCauley's museum in Houston) to do likewise and abandon any conversation that had not been concluded.

"If you will look through the window of the X-ray room," Andrea began, "you can see the portrait as it is being scanned and the Mc36 interpretation here on the screen." The computer was turned on and a straight green line appeared. "Mr. Newman has given me permission to tell you that the painting was acquired by the Newman Gallery several years ago in an estate sale, and was said to be a portrait of a contemporary of Charles I of England. The owner of the painting told them that Van Dyck completed it in 1634 when he was painter to the English court."

The X-ray technician started at the top left-hand corner of the canvas and scanned straight across, then came back in the opposite direction until the entire surface had been covered. As this was being done Andrea told her audience that the computer could complete a chemical analysis in three minutes that would ordinarily take eight hours.

A violet-colored line had appeared above the green one

on the screen, and the printer portion ticked off a series of five-digit numbers that were coded along with the color and configuration of the lines on the screen to indicate specific chemicals.

"The computer tells us that the pigment was suspended in egg white," Andrea said, "which is consistent with the type of paint Van Dyck would have used in 1634 . . ."

Suddenly, the green line became a series of inverted *vs*, and the printer added five new numbers. "Stop there a moment," Andrea said to the X-ray operator, who had trained the machine on the center of the beard. Andrea pointed to a green line on the small TV screen. "This, and the additional five-digit numbers tell us that a new chemical is present." Pausing dramatically, she said with a straight face, "The new chemical is titanium."

McCauley was the first to laugh, then the others joined him. It was an inside joke and they had all grasped the punch line—titanium was not used in paint until after 1920.

Obviously an enterprising forger had added the beard and the signature to the painting of an unknown artist from the same period as Van Dyck and tried to pass it off as genuine.

After the demonstration McCauley joined Andrea and led her toward the door. "They'll be all afternoon learning to use the computer," he said. "I thought we might go somewhere for a drink."

It was snowing again. Not the swirling splinters of ice that sometimes appeared far into the spring in Boston, but feathery flakes that accumulated in rounded mounds on buildings and bushes.

"I hope you don't mind walking," McCauley said. "I don't have much chance to walk in the snow in Houston."

She didn't mind, but she did not know where they were going until they stopped in front of the Prudential Tower.

In the lobby McCauley inserted a key in the lock of a private elevator and quickly they were whisked up fifty-two floors to a small "members only" lounge next to the Top of the Hub. The manager seated them in a secluded booth next to the window and almost instantly two Manhattans appeared before them.

If McCauley practiced economy nowhere else, he did with his words. There was no squandering small talk—no wasteful repetition of phrases. His questions were direct and personal and his response to Andrea's answers was attentive. He genuinely seemed to want to know all about her. By the time she had finished the first Manhattan she had told him about her undergraduate work at Radcliffe, the doctoral program at Harvard, and the offer of an apprenticeship in Italy.

As the afternoon lengthened, the streetlights came on. The city lay far beneath them, white and clean. The frozen trees on the Boston Common glittered like intricate crystal sculpture.

With a sign from McCauley the manager dispatched two waiters into the kitchen who quickly reappeared. One carried china and cutlery, the other a large tureen and a basket with chunks of French bread.

"The cook here makes the best bouillabaisse in Boston," McCauley said, filling Andrea's bowl. At the first whiff of the thick, steamy fish chowder, she realized she was famished.

During dinner it was McCauley who did most of the talking. In the same spare rhetoric he told her about his background in Texas. He made no apologies for his wealth or false claims to estheticism.

Long after the evening was past Andrea could recall their conversation as though it had been a class lecture and she had transcribed it and filed it away under plastic topic tabs, cross-indexed by subject and event:

McCAULEY ON HIS WEALTH
see also . . .
McCAULEY SELECTING THE WINE
Mc: My father had the pleasure of making the money. He and Toddie Lee Wynn, Clint Murcheson, and Sid Richardson were called the New Athenians . . .

A: Athenians?

Mc: Athens, Texas. They all came from there, and they were all in on the oil strike at Burkburnett. By the time I was in charge, all that was left to do was administrative.

A's NOTATION: Administrative and manipulative. His father may have started the McCauley fortune in oil in the '30s, but she had read that Clint McCauley, as a very young man in the '50s, had seen the potential in computers and converted a large share of company holdings to that burgeoning new industry.

McCAULEY ON ART COLLECTION
see also . . .
McCAULEY REACHING ACROSS THE TABLE TO TOUCH MY HAIR
Mc: I've never seen hair that color except in a Titian painting.

A: (No response—but the hair that fringed her forehead where his hand had been seemed to have developed nerve endings.)

Mc: I hedged earlier when you asked what I look for in selecting a painting. That's the quality . . . rarity.

A: Rarity is more important than beauty?

Mc: Your hair happens to be both, but yes.

A: Then it wouldn't matter what you collected. It could be coins, or bottle caps . . .

Mc: It has to have value. There are rare diseases, too.

A: By value, do you mean value to others . . . something other collectors would covet?

Mc: That's part of it. Onassis, for instance, collected

rare women. Not the most beautiful women, but beyond duplication. Unfortunately, the greatest pleasure is in acquiring.

A: The pleasure is the pursuit?

Mc: Exactly. Like tracking an elk. First you spot the spoor . . . then you wait. Patience is important. The thrill begins when you hear the rustle of a bush . . . then the antlers appear . . . finally the head and neck . . . but you wait for a clear shot at the chest. What's the matter, are you squeamish?

A: A little.

Mc: You think an elk should die a natural death?

A: It would be nice to think so.

Mc: Shooting is quick and clean. A natural death would be starvation, a pack of wolves, or a bear. Did you ever see what bear talons can do?

THE REST DELETED

A'S NOTATIONS: Granted, his heart would never stop nor his eyes fill with tears as hers did when she saw a magnificent painting, but he would recognize its value and the rarity of a genius that could produce such a thing. Isn't that kind of appreciation just as valid? Does it have to be emotional?

McCAULEY ON HIS MARRIAGE

see also . . .

McCAULEY ORDERING BRANDY

Mc: I didn't marry until I was thirty. My wife is the daughter of the late Senator Blackman. It didn't take us long to find out we had very few of the same appetites. But she tried to please me at first. She even took up painting when I began collecting . . . so we'd have something in common, she said. Of course there is no common ground there at all, but to her mind she was sharing something with me. However, a few years ago she decided she wanted to stay at the house in Palm Beach permanently and paint seascapes in the summer and entertain her political friends in the winter. She seems quite happy.

The tureen was empty, and Andrea had left only a few pieces of lobster shell in her bowl. She still felt a warm glow from the brandy when McCauley helped her on with her coat. He lifted her hair from beneath her collar and brushed her cheek with his lips as he did.

"I'll have someone call for my car," he said.

"If you still feel like walking, I live only a few blocks from here," Andrea suggested.

Outside it had stopped snowing, but a frozen mist moved diagonally in front of them, then swirled in the wake of a passing bus and changed direction. At Arlington Street they turned right onto Beacon and walked parallel with the Common Garden. The shallow pond was frozen solid and wore fresh scars inflicted by recent skaters. The benches spaced along the pathway were newly upholstered with cushions of snow.

McCauley took Andrea's arm and led her across the street under the awning of a dress shop. He put his hands on her shoulders and bent to kiss her. His lips were full and warm and moved lightly on hers. Weightlessly his hands rested on her shoulders until Andrea moved to close the space between them.

They stepped back onto the frozen sidewalk and taking McCauley's hand, Andrea led him through a shortcut to her apartment on Charles Street.

McCauley on making love

For once, Andrea did not catalogue the dialogue. If she had reduced the night to words they would have been—sensual . . . practiced . . . demanding—and giving . . . but only pleasure—not himself—not the part beyond the physical that she wanted. He was a sealed room. In time, she hoped she'd find the way inside.

In the morning when he asked her to accompany the Mc36 to Houston, to create her own department of restoration at the McCauley Museum, she had accepted with hardly a backward glance toward Italy. But that afternoon, the photograph in Wilkie Newman's office changed her mind.

She had seen it before but had never looked at it with such interest. In the photograph Newman stood on one side of a Giovanni Bellini painting of the *Madonna and Saints* (for which McCauley had paid an unprecedented price). McCauley stood on the other side; seated in front of him was Mrs. McCauley. She was a lovely, smiling lady in a chair that had tubular metal arms and rubber-rimmed wheels. Her eyes were like Andrea's sister Joy's—so full of forgiveness that it was impossible not to feel guilty under their gaze.

Roses arrived that afternoon from McCauley with a handwritten note asking Andrea to call. Enclosed was a printed card with half a dozen telephone numbers (one local, one in New York, one in Houston and the other three in different countries) all marked "Direct line."

Andrea left the next week for Florence without seeing McCauley again.

Chapter 5

Vittorio Sassetti left the small X-ray room and went into the reception area of the Accademia. "We need to place a call to Tom Daley at the McCauley Museum in Houston, Texas," he said to his wife.

Rosa did not look up from the letter she was typing, but called over her shoulder, "Andrea. What time is it now in Texas?"

Still in the laboratory where the portrait of David had been examined Andrea checked her watch. "Around four or five o'clock in the morning, I think." She unhooked the clamps of the X-ray scanner and lifted the painting down. Holding it carefully by the wooden frame, she carried it into her own office, placed it on an easel in front of her desk, then joined Vittorio in the reception room with Rosa.

"Of course, of course," Vittorio said, as though he had taken the time difference into consideration all along. "Later this afternoon we must make a call and ask the McCauley Museum to send their computer. *Cara*," he said to Andrea his arm around her shoulder, "perhaps you should be the one to talk to Signore Daley. Over the telephone, sometimes my English, it is not so good." His tone implied that it was somehow the fault of the telephone company that he could not always make himself understood.

Suddenly there was a nervous cough from the doorway that led into the hall. "Excuse me, Signore Sassetti," Luca, the guard, stammered.

Vittorio jumped at the sound of the young man's voice and quickly turned toward him.

Andrea rushed to her office and closed the door, blocking the view of the portrait of David that had been clearly visible in the reception area.

"The basement, sir."

"What about the basement?"

"It's *clean*. I cleaned it. You said I could go after . . ."

"Yes, yes. Then go, for heaven's sake." Vittorio motioned him out.

Andrea stood leaning against her office door, both hands still holding the knob behind her. How long, she wondered uneasily, had Luca been standing there?

In his eagerness to be out of the Accademia, Luca cut a corner too sharply into the great hall and collided with a mobile easel and its owner, a friend from student days.

"Luca! Take it easy! What the hell . . ."

A half-completed canvas clattered to the floor along with a tube of ocher and a half dozen various-sized brushes.

"*Scusi*, Gino." Luca bent to pick up the brushes and paint.

Gino Corsini examined the canvas. "No harm done," he said.

Luca glanced at it, too. The painting was another of Gino's pallid, uninspired landscapes. Luca's appraisal of Gino's work was always the same—good technique, unoriginal concept. Gino had a brother who did very well in the black market. Luca could not understand why Gino continued to try to paint when there was a place for him in a thriving family business. Luca had given up painting just to be a museum guard, and he knew he was much more talented than Gino.

But he could not solve Gino's problems. He had his own to attend to. Waving to his friend he hurried down the basement stairs and out the door. He unfastened the chain that secured his new yellow Vespa to the bike rack and rode up the narrow brick alley to Via Ricasoli, where he wove in and out of the heavy traffic.

He was still embarrassed at having been caught sleeping on the job by his boss, Vittorio Sassetti, but his chagrin blossomed into bravado in the open air. I should have quit, Luca thought. I should have quit and told him what he could do with his Accademia. But Luca knew that he would not quit. He needed the money, and he usually liked his job. It made him feel important. He especially liked being trained by the *polizia* to use a gun. And the uniform with the gold braid on the jacket and trouser legs! He loved the uniform.

But the Vespa was expensive. The payments took most of his salary. There was no money left to rent his own apartment, to get away from his father's constant disapproval.

Gino Corsini, he thought, was crazy not to work for his brother. Gino's brother Pietro Corsini, due to his connections with the dockworkers in Genoa, had a slick operation. He was not someone you would want as an enemy; Luca knew that Gino's brother Pietro carried both a gun and a knife. Pietro knew how the system worked.

Dabbling in the black market was like belonging to a secret society. Nearly everyone Luca knew was involved to some extent. From time to time Luca had made deliveries for Gino's brother to the Mercato Nuovo, the Straw Market. There, merchants sold leather goods, straw baskets, and souvenirs to the tourists out the front of their wooden stalls, and sold black market cigarettes and crates of citrus fruit to the Florentines behind the stalls. Everyone Luca knew bought or sold on the black market—everyone but Gino Corsini, who kept plodding along with his palette and paintbrush. *Even* Gino, Luca amended. Where does he think the money Pietro shells out for his tuition comes from?

Luca made a sharp left into an open piazza. At the opposite end he noticed three college-age girls in jeans and T-shirts. They were eating ice cream cones, their backpacks resting against a stone wall that circled a small fountain. He turned off the Vespa's motor and slowed down.

"*Buon giorno*, ladies," he announced, skidding to a stop, using the sole of his shoe as a break.

"Hiya, cowboy," replied the cute one, who wore an orange T-shirt with an advertisement for an American brand of beer. "What are you? Some kind of fancy Italian doorman?"

"Police." Luca smiled at her, putting the kickstand down and getting off the Vespa. "Secret Service," he said with an exaggerated wink.

"Some secret in that uniform." The girl laughed.

While the other two girls stood by, bored, Luca and the one with the chocolate ice cream cone made a try at conversation that was a mixture of fractured Italian on the girl's part, limited English on Luca's, and enthusiastic sign language from both of them.

Luca eyed her appreciatively. I'll bet I could get her to come with me, he thought. When there were three girls together, he could usually snag one of them. It was hard to separate two—but three was different.

Unfortunately, he had no place to take her.

As he got back on the Vespa, he reached out and touched the beer bottle stencilled on the orange T-shirt.

"Sexy," he said, then grabbed her ice cream cone and rode off with it. He entered the street, picked up speed, and thought, I've got to get my own apartment.

For a while he rode on toward his father's house, thinking how close he had come to losing his job. And now with the physical distance between himself and Vittorio Sassetti, he began to puzzle over his boss's strange behavior. He pieced together the fragments of conversation he had heard and tried to remember what stood behind the door Signorina Perkins had been so anxious to close.

Suddenly, he threw the soggy tip of the cone into the gutter, made a U-turn and headed in the opposite direction. Gino might not be interested in his brother Pietro's illegal business, but Luca was. Luca would check with Pietro to see if he had more deliveries he could make, and perhaps, Luca thought, *he* had some information that would interest Pietro.

As he recrossed the piazza, he looked back and waved to the girl in the orange shirt who was now strapping on her backpack.

"Hey, sexy," she yelled, "you owe me an ice cream cone!"

Late in the afternoon Rosa placed the call to Houston. She nodded in response to the answer she was getting from the speaker on the other end of the line.

"Well? What is happening?" Vittorio asked, tapping a finger on the desk.

"Tom Daley is not there. His secretary says he is with Signore McCauley at the ranch."

"Then call him there," Vittorio said impatiently.

Andrea paced the small room nervously, anxious to complete the call. She had spent the afternoon concluding some earlier tests. Then she had carefully wrapped the portrait of David in cotton batting, sealed it in a thick plastic envelope and locked it away in the basement safe.

"The secretary says I should leave a message, and Mr. Daley will return the call," Rosa reported.

"Ask for the number at the ranch," Vittorio insisted.

"She doesn't have the number. No one at the museum has Signore McCauley's private number."

"Dio mio!" Vittorio slapped his forehead with the heel of his hand in exasperation.

Of course it could wait a few more hours, Andrea thought. But she knew the agitated state Vittorio would be in until they had actually talked to Tom Daley about using the Mc36 computer to run the final tests on the portrait of David. She reached in her billfold and took out the note that had come with McCauley's roses last spring in Boston. "Here, Rosa, try this," Andrea said, copying the number from the card onto a note pad.

Rosa looked up at the younger woman in surprise.

"I did some work for Clint McCauley in Boston. It's a direct line."

Rosa thanked Tom Daley's secretary and hung up. She dialed the new number, and when it began to ring, vacated her chair at the desk and handed the phone to Andrea. Gratefully, Andrea sat down, not sure how her knees would behave if she heard Clint McCauley's voice again.

McCauley's ranch was on an island. More exactly, it *was* an island—a boomerang-shaped expanse of clean, flat beach and soft, grassy sand dunes that lay off the Texas coastline. To the north, the sun-bleached buildings of Galveston could be seen across the bay. To the south, the offshore rigs of the McCauley Oil Company stood like amphibious giants in the Gulf of Mexico, flashing their warning lights to unwary ships and planes.

The ranch house was a comfortable, one-story white frame building that rambled in a U-shape and enclosed, on three sides, a flagstone patio and an Olympic-sized pool. Beyond the pool, fifty yards of white sand sloped down to the shallow floor of the Gulf.

This was one of the five places McCauley could truly call home. There was his estate in Palm Beach where his wife lived (and he rarely visited), a villa near Florence, a ski lodge in Gstaad, and a town house in London. But because his corporate headquarters were in Houston, most of his time was spent at the ranch.

Tom Daley, in a business suit, sat stiffly at the side of the pool in a chair designed for lounging. His nervous system could not adapt to lounging under most circumstances, and certainly not today. He had been asked to wait and meet with Clint McCauley privately.

Behind him, the chef and his crew were clearing away the remains of a ranch-style breakfast they had served to thirty people. The guests had been invited to meet the new chancellor of Crockett University, where McCauley was a heavy contributor.

Most everyone was gone now. McCauley's launch had taken some of them back to port in Galveston. Others had boarded his helicopter and had probably already landed at the heliport on top of the McCauley building in Houston.

Besides Daley, one other guest remained, the First Vice President of the Houston Junior League, a stunning recent divorcée. In a colder climate she might have gone unnoticed. Her pale skin, blond hair, and pale blue eyes might have blended to colorlessness. But the daily application of tanning lotion and forty-five minutes in the Texas sun kept her well-constructed body the color of burnished pine. Her name was Bettina Huffines, and at the moment, clad in a white bikini, she climbed onto the diving board and posed, waiting until she was sure she had Clint McCauley's attention.

McCauley paused at the other end of the pool, having

completed ten laps, and glanced in her direction as she pressed her palms together above her head, bounced once on the board, bent forward, and slid neatly into the water.

Daley watched her smooth, sleek movements beneath the surface. However, his appreciation of her grace was no more than he would have bestowed on a seal or an otter or any other accomplished sea mammal. His thoughts were elsewhere.

Daley's refusal of an after-breakfast swim (he was secretly terrified of the water) had been met with a shrug from his boss. "We'll talk after I've done twenty laps," McCauley had said, simply postponing what the curator of the McCauley Museum knew was inevitable. He was going to be fired.

The whole Texas experience had been a fiasco. The culture shock between Boston and Houston was just too great for him to overcome. True, the credentials that had gotten him the job in the first place were not wholly his own. He had dipped pretty deeply into Andrea Perkins' research when she was his assistant at the Museum in Cambridge. Without her knowledge, he had submitted with his application to McCauley a paper she had written, which stated that the artists of the Renaissance had formulated their attitudes toward art and music from Plato and other Greek philosophers. McCauley had been especially impressed with the closing sentence: "Art was not merely a matter of pleasure, it had the power to heal the sick, to move the 'whole man' of the humanists, to affect him morally and spiritually."

But beyond that, was Daley's inadaquacy in the social aspects of his job. Wealthy Texans, in their eagerness for culture, could accept someone with a background different from their own only if the person's talents could be displayed on a stage—a conductor, a ballerina, a tenor. But Daley had only himself to present to them, and he came off

42

as effete and flustered.

He watched Clint McCauley's concentrated breast-stroke. How did McCauley do it—a man in his fifties? He sliced through the water in a straight line, never listing to the side of the pool, swimming straight ahead as though he were being pulled at the end of a rope. He had made his displeasure with Daley's performance as curator quite clear. This was a famous McCauley technique: Terminate an unsatisfactory employee somewhere away from his place of business so there was no last minute chance to rearrange the books, hire or fire other employees, in fact, no opportunity to further make his presence known in any way. Even the final act of cleaning out his desk was not permitted. Its contents would be found in a cardboard box on the back seat of a rented car as he watched his company-owned vehicle being driven away.

When the phone rang, Daley jumped, Ms. Huffines frowned, and McCauley turned, annoyed, toward the unexpected sound. Since fewer than a half dozen people in the whole world had McCauley's private number, he assumed the call was for him and climbed out of the pool, grabbing a towel from the back of a chair.

Seconds later, a butler, dressed casually in jeans and a checked shirt, came out carrying a cordless phone and put it on a table at the pool's edge.

"The caller asked for Mr. Daley," the butler said, handing the phone to McCauley.

Daley leaped to his feet, looking confused. He didn't even know the telephone number himself. How could someone be calling him here?

McCauley handed the phone to the curator with a quizzical look. He turned his back and rubbed his wet hair vigorously with the towel, then walked to the side of the pool and talked quietly to the young woman who was wrapping herself in a terrycloth robe.

From the Texas end of the transatlantic call there was very little comment. Then Daley said, "—I imagine it could be arranged, but would you mind explaining it to Mr. McCauley yourself?" Daley put the receiver down on the lounge chair and scurried to Clint McCauley's side. "It's Andrea Perkins in Florence. Something about the Mc36 computer. I thought you should speak with her."

McCauley, unhurried, went to the phone. "Andrea, how nice to talk with you again." His voice conveyed only the pleasure of an affectionate business acquaintance.

"Hello, Clint."

"How can we help you?"

"Vittorio and I have come across what we think may be a very important painting."

"It must be important if more than your own excellent ability is needed."

"It's passed every test we've been able to perform here, but we need the signature analyzed, and wondered if it would be possible to use the Mc36. Of course we'd be pleased to have Tom Daley assist us, if he'd care to come."

"Only if the invitation includes me, too."

"Of course, if you can spare the time."

He gave her the date when they would arrive, then added, "It's been far too long since I've been in Florence."

"And one more thing," Andrea said, "I know I don't have to say this, but we don't want word to leak out to the press or even to other museums just yet. Not until we are sure of what it is."

"Naturally. My best to Vittorio and Rosa."

"We'll see you soon, then. Good-bye."

"Good-bye."

McCauley hung up the phone. His eyes were on Ms. Huffines who was posing prettily on a banana lounge, but his thoughts were on a girl six thousand miles away.

"Bettina," he said, crossing to her, taking her hand and gently pulling her to her feet. "Tom Daley will take you back on the launch. It should be waiting at the dock by now."

Bettina Huffines looked surprised, then injured, then resigned, and went into one of the cabañas to change.

Long after Daley had taken the reluctant Ms. Huffines to the launch, both men were still thinking of the telephone call.

Tom Daley grinned, the warm water of the gulf spraying his face. Andrea Perkins had unwittingly given him a reprieve by confiding the discovery of the painting to him. To insure the secrecy she had requested, McCauley would have to let him remain as curator until after the painting was examined. He did not fool himself that his employment would extend beyond that, but in the meantime, maybe he would come up with something else.

Clint McCauley, in jeans and shirtless, walked along the white beach. The only sound was the soft lapping of the surf as it reached and receded on the sand. Then from behind a row of dunes at the rear of the island came the angry snort of one of his prize Santa Gertrudis bulls. A snake, McCauley thought absently. The ranch hands would probably find the stomped remains in the barn.

What had she found? he wondered. He knew Andrea's field of expertise was Botticelli, Michelangelo, and Titian. There was no question that she thought her discovery was important or she would not have called—not after all this time.

His thoughts were of Florence, and his memories were of Boston as he started back toward the house. The sun was beginning to burn into his shoulders, and he sat in the shadow of the porch a long while, watching the moving reflection of the water from the pool as it played against the porch's ceiling.

In the servants' lounge at Clint McCauley's villa in Florence, a man in polished boots crossed the room and turned down the sound on the TV. "It's too loud," he said to the cook and two kitchen maids, who were watching the evening news.

The man picked up a copy of *Galoppo E Trotto* (the Italian racing form) from a swivel chair in the corner, glanced briefly at the headlines, then dropped the news of yesterday's races in the wastebasket. This man did not spend his money on the horses. He would need it later on if he was ever going to get out of Italy.

He sat, propping his boots on the edge of a desk, and took his favorite book from the center drawer. He spread Carlos Baker's biography of Ernest Hemingway across his knees. It fell open at a page of illustrations. There was a smiling Hemingway kneeling beside the carcass of a buffalo he had felled on the Serengeti Plain. A rifle was propped upright against the broad chest of the animal—a symbol of victory. On the same page was a picture of the writer and his wife, Pauline, smiling, kneeling beside the body of a lion, its massive chin flattened on the hard ground. One paw, which minutes before had prowled noiselessly through the tall grass, was extended toward the camera, clumsy and flat.

The man liked the chapters on hunting. But he particularly liked the part of the book where, when things got dull in America, Hemingway went off to get involved in the Spanish Civil War. He liked the words Hemingway had invented to describe the sound of a rifle firing: "tacrong, carong, craang"—and the machine guns, "rong, cararong, rong rong." And he understood when the book said

Hemingway had been "attracted by danger, death, great deeds." They "revived and rejuvenated him."—Yes—he understood that.

He was annoyed when the telephone on the desk rang. He closed the book and let his boots crash to the floor.

The call was brief and specific. There were no pauses for questions, no openings for disagreements. It ended with the admonition: ". . . be especially careful to keep track of the girl. Find out where she lives and what her schedule is." And then the line went dead.

Carlos Baker's book was put back in the desk drawer.

The man leaned back in his swivel chair, then thoughtfully sighted down his finger at a moth fluttering in the light of the desk lamp. "Tacrong, carong, craang," he said softly to himself.

Chapter 6

When Andrea left the Accademia it was dark, and the muted fog had returned. Home-bound traffic had thinned when she drove her red Alfa Romeo onto Via Ricasoli. Instead of going directly to the Albion Hotel where she lived, she pulled to the curb two blocks down in front of a large, intimidating stone building with a lighted sign over the door that said *Polizia*.

Captain Aldo Balzani of the Florence Police Department looked at the file folders on his desk. The top one was marked ASSAULT, the second, MURDER, the third, KIDNAPPING. There were more folders under those. Balzani sighed, and opened the top one, determined to go through the meager facts one more time.

The police captain's patience was a virtue that had been nourished in the city where he grew up—New Orleans, Louisiana. To hurry for any reason in the languid humidity of the Delta's Crescent City was counterproductive.

Balzani had been born in Florence, but when he was ten years old, his mother died and he was sent to America to live with his grandmother. She consoled the small boy as best she could and expressed her love and sympathy in her cooking. Aldo grew strong and content, eating the excellent Creole food and the ever-present staple of the Italian household, pasta. When he reached college age he was awarded an athletic scholarship to Tulane University, where he was starting halfback for the "Green Wave." He also joined the opera club.

From his earliest days with his grandmother, she had insisted that he study music, and he was surprised to find when he matured that he was a pretty fair baritone. His last year at Tulane he was featured soloist in a poorly attended opera club recital where he sang excerpts from Rossini's *The Barber of Seville*.

After receiving a master's degree in political science he was promised an appointment on the staff of the lieutenant governor (a football enthusiast). Balzani made plans to move to Baton Rouge in the fall after graduation, but fate—in the form of a student-exchange scholarship—stepped in. The scholarship was not his, but Lili Matucci's, the soprano from the opera club to whom he was engaged. Lili was invited to spend a year in the chorus of the Florentine Opera Company. With the summer to spare, Aldo went along.

Once there, he found the many members of his rediscovered family to be warm and cheerful. His father, whom he had seen only sporadically during the years in America, urged him to stay in Italy—at least a year or two. From the beginning the thought had been tempting. There would be no problem in finding a position on the police force, his father, the police chief, had assured him. The summer had ripened like the vineyards.

Aldo and Lili saw each other almost constantly during the winter season and they continued to talk of marriage. But when she returned with the chorus from a summer schedule of concerts in Milan, she calmly told Aldo she was going to marry the assistant manager of the opera company.

Aldo Balzani was stunned. His heart was broken. But

he found consolation in rediscovering Florence, and adjusting to the position he had accepted with the police force, which was to lead to his assignment in the detective division.

He had spread the contents of the file folder marked ASSAULT on his desk when his office door was opened by a uniformed policeman. With him was a stunning red-haired lady.

"Captain, the signorina asked to speak to someone about secret surveillance," the policeman said, stepping aside so that Andrea could enter the office.

Captain Balzani, in a brown business suit, stood behind the desk to greet her. "*Avanti*," he said in welcome, and offered her a battered-looking wooden chair.

"*Grazie.*" Andrea had tried to explain in Italian to the policeman why she was there, but secret surveillance was not what she meant. "What's the word for . . ." she said in English as she smoothed her skirt under her. The ancient folding chair pinched her little finger as she sat and made her cry out.

"I'm sorry, ma'am," Balzani said in lazy English. "That chair's got jaws like an alligator. Here. Let me see your hand."

Andrea could not have been more surprised if he had spoken to her in Chinese. He looked like a travel-poster photo of what an Italian detective should be. He was slim, muscular, with brown eyes, olive skin, black curly hair, a slightly hooked nose—and he was speaking to her in what was unmistakably an American Southern accent.

"It didn't break the skin, but you might want to put a Band Aid on it when you get home," Captain Balzani said, standing beside her, letting go of her hand.

Noting her reaction, he mentioned that he had lived in New Orleans. Then, seated at his desk again, he asked how the Police Department of Florence could be of service to her.

Andrea introduced herself and explained her association with the Accademia and then added, "Secret surveillance wasn't what I meant. Just . . . surveillance. I wanted to know how well patrolled the area around the Accademia is."

"Has there been some trouble?"

"No, nothing like that. Of course we have our own guards and the security system, but I just wondered how much additional protection we get from the city police."

Balzani briefly explained to her the routes and routine of the two patrolmen assigned to the area. When he finished, he noticed she was frowning. "Was there some special reason . . . ?"

"You see, we have a valuable painting." She paused, not wanting to confide even to a detective what she and Vittorio suspected about the portrait of David.

"Yes, ma'am?"

"I mean we have a number of paintings . . ." She shifted uncomfortably in the chair. Of *course* we have a number of paintings, she thought, feeling foolish. It's a museum.

Balzani waited for her to continue. When she didn't, he said, "The private security service employed by all the museums in Florence does excellent work."

"Yes, but this painting can't be catalogued yet and can't be stored in the vault." She was beginning to feel sorry she had come. "I just wanted to request a little extra attention from the police for the next week or so." She stood to leave.

"I'll see that the assigned patrolmen are alerted," the detective captain said, walking with her to the door.

"After we have examined the painting and coded it into

51

the security computer, I'll let you know. Good night, Captain."

"Good night, Miss Perkins."

With less enthusiasm than before, Captain Balzani went back to work on the assault case. Too bad, he thought, that there weren't more interruptions in his life like Miss Perkins.

The lobby of the Albion Hotel appeared to be empty, but there was no absence of noise. From the large television set in the corner the Prime Minister was soberly warning his 57.5 million fellow Italians that their country's recession was deepening. And in the small office behind the U-shaped reception desk, Andrea could hear the hotel proprietor, Leo Fozzi, overriding the TV in an agitated telephone conversation.

Andrea crossed the worn green carpet, stood in Fozzi's line of vision and rang the desk-top service bell. Fozzi's face seemed to close like a shuttered window when he saw her. He muttered something into the phone and hung up.

He slipped his composure on with his striped jacket and came into the lobby to greet her. Andrea took a step away from him. His greetings were always exuberant, and it took some maneuvering to avoid his hugs and kisses.

"Is there any mail for me?" Andrea asked.

"Sì, signorina, I will get it." Fozzi gave her a radiant smile that implied that performing the smallest service for her was his greatest pleasure in life. He hurried behind the counter and reached into the mailbox with her name on it.

Leo Fozzi was a short man with patent-leather-shod feet that looked too small to support the bulk of the rest of his body. He gave a great deal of time and effort to his appearance—with negative results. His hair, which he tinted himself, was an eggplant shade just short of black.

But he considered himself irresistible to the ladies. Andrea had learned the first day she registered at the hotel never to walk upstairs in front of him.

He turned now, and with a bow handed Andrea a magazine, two bills, and the weekly letter from home. The letter, she knew, would be filled with an account of the macramé wall hanging that was her sister Joy's current project. Andrea thanked the hotel proprietor and started for her room.

Leo Fozzi stood and watched Andrea's hips and legs appreciatively as she walked up the stairs. When she turned the corner of the corridor, he went back into the lobby, pausing briefly to straighten one of the pictures that hung near the door.

The walls of the Albion Hotel's two-story lobby were filled with paintings done by students from the Accademia. Fozzi boasted that his hotel was considered a gallery by the students who competed for showings there. He sometimes sold their paintings to guests of the hotel; and if the age of the painting or the signature on the canvas was not always exactly as Fozzi represented it, it did not matter. The buyer went away happy, believing what Fozzi told him.

Fozzi went behind the desk and picked up the phone again. He dialed a familiar number and stood listening as the phone at the other end rang and was answered by Gino Corsini.

"Let me speak with Pietro again," Fozzi said.

When Pietro Corsini came to the phone, Leo Fozzi continued the conversation which had been interrupted by Andrea's arrival. Their discussion related to the unexpected business proposition Fozzi had received earlier that evening. Fozzi told his sometime partner only the bare bones of the plan and suggested that they meet in the hotel's storage area in the garage the following morning at 7:15. Important as their meeting would be, there was no need to disrupt routine. Fozzi—a man of habit—was always in the garage storage area at 7:15 in the morning to check supplies.

Chapter 7

Time had a different dimension in Italy. It did not flow, but collected in a motionless pool, or so it seemed to Andrea the week between the discovery of the portrait and the arrival of the Mc36 computer.

Her thoughts seemed to revolve exclusively around the fact that the computer was being accompanied not only by Tom Daley, the curator of the Houston museum, but by Clint McCauley as well.

She had known McCauley had a villa in Florence. The telephone number there had been on the card with the other direct lines that had come with the roses.

She tried not to imagine what it would be like to see him again, but at unexpected moments she found herself remembering the icy wind in their faces that night as they walked toward Beacon Hill, and later, the warmth of his breath on her neck. At such moments she would look for something that needed her immediate attention—a list of supplies to be ordered, a damaged painting to be repaired—but usually she would find herself glancing at the calendar again and wondering if the days would ever pass.

Her first and last self-imposed task each day that week was to check on the safety of the painting. This would have been no problem if she had put it in the Accademia's vault, but that would entail confiding their secret to the intra-city computer.

The Uffizi Gallery, the Nazionale, the Pitti Palace, the Accademia—all the major museums and galleries in Florence—had interconnecting computer terminals. Their inventory—each individual art object—was coded and given a number, then the information about each one was fed into and digested by the computer. It provided an easily accessible cross-reference for scholars, artists, writers, and museum personnel. But until the portrait of David had been examined and identified, Vittorio and Andrea decided to store it in the basement safe where paintings that were waiting to be catalogued were held. Each day Andrea checked the safe, and each day the plastic envelope with its contents was exactly where they had placed it. But just seeing that it was still there was not enough. Andrea would touch the slick plastic and gently squeeze it until she felt the firmness of the picture's frame beneath the cotton batting that surrounded it. And still she worried.

The full moon had risen above the Tuscan hills and lit the steep winding road to Clint McCauley's villa almost as brightly as did the retractable headlights of his limousine.

During the week, McCauley's secretary in Houston had called the Accademia to invite Vittorio and Rosa Sassetti and Andrea to join him for dinner the day after his arrival, stating that a driver would be sent for them. Now, dressed in evening clothes, the three of them sat together in the glove-leather-upholstered seats of the custom-designed automobile.

"This limousine cost a bundle," the driver, a young man in a cowboy hat with a turkey-feather band told them. He was Bud McCauley—Clint McCauley's nephew and caretaker of the villa. "It was made to order in Milan at the

56

Alfa Romeo plant and has an emergency telephone, puncture-proof tires, an automatic fire extinguisher, computerized map display, and listen . . ." Bud flipped on a siren that grew in an instant from a guttural whirr to a piercing scream before he turned it off again. "All this special equipment adds about nine hundred pounds—but watch how she can take this hill!" Bud stepped on the accelerator and the car lifted up the incline like a jet on takeoff.

"There is an especially sharp curve ahead," Vittorio said nervously.

"Yeah, I know. I've learned this road pretty well," Bud said, slowing down, having made his point. "I had to talk Uncle Clint into buying it. The money wasn't the problem. He just wasn't convinced that he needed a bulletproof car."

The three passengers in the back seat exchanged knowing glances, aware of the danger to celebrities and wealthy residents and visitors in Italy.

The limousine stopped in front of a tall, curved-topped gate which had been formed into a fluid design of fish frolicking in silvery curls of wrought-iron water. At young McCauley's press of a remote-control button on the dashboard, a metal Neptune released his trident that held the two sides together. They glided noiselessly open. Mounted on a high spiked fence next to the gate and partially concealed by a low-hanging branch of an olive tree was a surveillance TV camera.

Because of the lush plantings on both sides of the cobblestone drive, the villa was not visible until they were only a few yards from the ornate porte cochere where the limousine purred to a stop.

Andrea followed Vittorio and Rosa toward the wide front steps. The door of the villa was flanked by black marble griffins—their eagle faces skyward, wings half opened, ready to lift their lion bodies from the pedestals and hover above the cypress trees.

The villa was two stories of pink stucco, recently sandblasted and repainted. The white rococo trim was as spotless as it had been two hundred or so years earlier when the structure was completed.

The opulent villa and the bulletproof limousine suggested the possessions of a slick-haired Sicilian Don—which Andrea knew was about 180 degrees from the man waiting for them in the foyer.

If Andrea had imagined that time had painted her memory of McCauley's eyes bluer, his face a deeper tan, his manner more gracious than it was, she was mistaken. He was exactly as he had been last winter in Boston.

He greeted Rosa and Vittorio, and then cordially turned to Andrea.

"And you, young lady," he said, taking her hand in his cool fingers, "are the one responsible for all this excitement, I understand."

If he had any unasked questions about why she had left Boston without seeing him again—if he had used the Mc36 computer as an excuse to see her again—there was no hint of it in his manner. He had kissed the hand of Rosa Sassetti with the same amount of fervor he had shown with Andrea. Her heart felt as though it had dropped somewhere beneath her rib cage.

McCauley took her arm, and, followed by Vittorio and Rosa, led her across the black and white marble squares of the foyer past a nine-foot-tall bronze statue of a nude nymph holding an urn that constantly poured water into a gold fish pond at her feet. In the *salone* a fire blazed and crackled confidently in the fireplace. On each side of it were comfortable, modern couches. Tom Daley sat on one of them, holding a cut-crystal highball glass.

Andrea greeted him with restrained courtesy and sat at

the opposite end of the couch. Daley had always reminded her of pictures she had seen of Oscar Wilde—the full, delicate mouth, the large, slightly tilted head, the graceful hand that when he spoke rested at his throat as though he were checking his own pulse.

A girl in a black uniform moved silently about the room, offering drinks and trays of canapés.

The conversation began with a discussion of the expansion plans of the McCauley Museum. As they talked, Daley's sparrow-colored eyes darted away when they accidentally made contact with Andrea's. He undoubtedly did not want to be reminded of the inordinate amount of his work she had done for him when they were associates at the museum in Cambridge. Andrea was no more eager for his company than he was for hers.

When the maid had left and closed the door, McCauley turned to Andrea, smiling, and said, "Now are you going to tell us about this marvelous painting of yours?"

She told them about the portrait of David, the meeting with the priest, her suspicions when she began to clean the canvas, and the thorough testing she had given it.

Through her story, McCauley sat listening to her intently. Halfway through the recital, Daley's mouth began to form a tentative smirk that was full-blown when she finished.

"Andrea, my dear, I must warn you," he said archly, "I approach your extraordinary find with skepticism." He launched into some of the reasons she herself had given Vittorio for doubting that Michelangelo had actually painted it. Daley ended by stating his opinion that even the Sistine Ceiling was primarily the work of apprentices. "It was done by committee," he said, his fingers fluttering at his throat, "like Shakespeare's plays."

He can't be serious, Andrea thought, but he looked deadly earnest, adding that he planned to write a book to support his thesis.

"But you mustn't be disappointed if it's a fake," Daley said, throwing his head back and tracing his Adam's apple with a long graceful finger. "You'll hardly be the first to make a mistake . . ."

"Even the McCauley Museum has made a few," McCauley said in a tone and with a glance that seemed to freeze Daley's face.

At that moment there was a discreet rap at the door and a tuxedoed servant came in and spoke softly to McCauley, then retreated.

"Dinner," McCauley said, standing and reaching a hand out to Andrea. Bud, who had been seated in a chair outside the *salone*, followed them toward the dining room. Although McCauley invited his nephew to join them for dinner, Bud refused, saying he still got hungry on "Texas time" and had had a steak before driving to Florence. He added that a Peroni beer sounded better than the pasta and clam sauce and headed for the kitchen in search of one.

When they were seated, before the inevitable shoptalk could pick up full speed, Rosa made an attempt to derail it. Rosa's only interest in art was that it paid her husband's salary as curator, and her own as his secretary—which made it possible for them to live in a modern apartment building with a view of the Arno on one side and the Piazza Santa Croce on the other. "We were impressed with your new limousine, Signore McCauley," she said.

"The limousine is Bud's toy." McCauley laughed. "He's been playing bodyguard ever since I was kidnapped last year."

"Kidnapped?" Daley turned, fork in midair.

"Two of the major industries in Italy are the black market and kidnapping," McCauley answered matter-of-factly.

"Who was it," Andrea asked, "the Red Brigades?"

60

"No, just a couple of local tough guys. One of them worked in the vineyard here on the grounds of the villa."

"But, what . . . ?" asked someone at the table. "But how . . . ?" asked someone else.

"I managed to escape," McCauley said. "I more or less outlasted them." McCauley paused for a sip of wine. "They were both drinking quite a lot of Chianti while we waited for the ransom to be delivered and I kept them talking . . . mostly about auto racing, as I remember, which seemed to interest them. My Italian is fair," he said to the group in general, then looked up as his nephew came through from the kitchen with a can of beer. "Not as good as Bud's," he added, grinning at the younger man, who acknowledged the comment and went out to the open veranda outside the dining room, "but then he has the advantage of living here most of the year. At any rate, after we had been in this shabby hotel room for several hours, one of the guys made a trip to the bathroom, and while he was gone, I managed to get the gun away from the other one."

"You were lucky they didn't both have guns," Vittorio said.

"Actually, they did," McCauley said. "But I'm a pretty fair shot. I've been bird hunting since I was a kid. When the bathroom door opened, I fired at the guy's wrist. The gun fell to the floor, and he fell back into the bathroom. I closed the door and pushed a heavy dresser in front of it, figuring that he was in no condition for furniture moving."

"But didn't the other man try to stop you?" Andrea asked.

"Well, in order to get his gun in the first place," McCauley said with the hint of a chuckle, "I had to hit him over the head with a wine bottle, so he missed the last part. With him lying on the floor and the other one trapped in the bathroom, I just walked out of the apartment."

No one at the dinner table spoke for a moment. Then Rosa said, "It seems strange that I don't recall reading about any of this in the newspaper."

"I never reported it to the police," McCauley said, smiling. "That's the kind of story the press loves, and I didn't want someone more skillful than those two to get the idea of doing an encore. Those clowns were amateurs, but there are some pretty accomplished criminals in Florence these days."

Andrea thought McCauley was the most self-sufficient man she had ever known. Was it possible that he simply did not need anyone else in his life?

After the kitchen was closed, the man sat in the servants' lounge polishing his boots with a dish towel.

He had overheard the dinner conversation about the kidnapping. McCauley had been right about *one* thing. The two that were sent to do the job were amateurs. If he had gone himself, McCauley would never have escaped.

He wadded the cloth into a ball and threw it into a corner. Most of the servants were gathered around the large color TV watching an American movie that had been clumsily dubbed in Italian.

Those two idiots were lucky they left town without coming back to the villa. They at least had that much sense.

He sighted down his finger with one eye at a character on the television screen. "Tacrong, carong, craang . . ." he said to himself, and thought of a night in another country when he had killed a man. It was in a barroom. He had made a bet with a stranger. He no longer recalled what the bet had been about, but the stakes were his pistol against the stranger's silver belt buckle. He won and the stranger reneged, so he shot and killed him. There was no more to it than that.

He had always been "revived and rejuvenated," as the Hemingway biography put it, by "danger, death, great deeds." Shooting a man because he welshed on a bet might not qualify as a "great deed" to some, but a great deed was what you chose to call it. And it had been a matter of honor.

He hated Florence . . . he hated Italy . . . he hated the man who paid his salary. There was a way, and he thought he had found it, to get enough money to leave. He went outside and leaned against the wall, out of range of the surveillance camera trained on the kitchen door, and reviewed his plan.

Chapter 8

"The almond flavor comes from apricot pits," McCauley told Tom Daley, who had lavishly complimented the Amaretto and now held his glass up to the butler for a refill.

The butler topped off the other glasses also, then put a log on the dwindling fire and discreetly left the room, silently closing the door to the *salone* behind him.

The after-dinner conversation had principally concerned the setting up of the Mc36 and agreeing on a schedule for examining the portrait of David. "Please, if you'll excuse us," McCauley said when the arrangements had been made, "there is something I'd like to show Miss Perkins in the library. Do help yourselves to more Amaretto."

Surprised, Andrea let him help her to her feet, then followed him through the foyer to a large oak-paneled room. Bookshelves lined three walls, and on the fourth stood an antique enameled credenza. McCauley went to it, opened the top drawer and took out a small portrait of a young Renaissance beauty in a gold frame. "You remember this," he said, handing it to Andrea.

It was the Arnoldi painting she had restored for the Newman Gallery and which McCauley had purchased from them.

Andrea studied the painting silently, then looked up at him quizzically, but he made no comment. Instead, he said, "What do you plan to do when you leave Florence?"

Teach again, she supposed, she told him, but she had no definite plans. She held out the Arnoldi miniature to him.

"No," he said, pushing it gently back to her, "I want you to keep it."

She was stunned. "I . . . I couldn't."

"You'd be doing me a favor," he said, smiling at her.

"Why?"

"Because," he said, taking her chin in his hand, "the girl in the painting has the same big honest eyes that you do." He grinned at her. "Eyes the color of Coke bottles, and I don't like the feeling of loss I have everytime I come across the picture unexpectedly." He kissed her lightly on the cheek, then took her by the arm. "We'd better be getting back, I suppose."

The stem of Andrea's resolve, nurtured so carefully for almost a year, wilted dangerously and shriveled like a snapdragon after the first frost. McCauley paused at the door before entering the *salone* and said to Andrea, "If you'll have dinner with me tomorrow night, I have a suggestion about your career." He turned the knob of the door but before opening it he took her arm again, and she was acutely aware of the slight roughness of his fingers through the chiffon sleeve of her dress.

"Yes. Yes, I'd like that," she heard herself saying.

Inside she could tell there had been a quarrel. And though Tom Daley's Italian was no better than Vittorio's English, they had understood each other well enough to disagree violently. Vittorio's face beneath his frown was now a deep red, and Daley had struck a smug Wildean pose—his head to one side, his fingers placed gracefully at his throat.

"Andrea," Vittorio said, standing up, "Signore Daley

has just made an interesting comment." He obviously was struggling to keep his composure. "He said that what we identified as the Medici Medallion was probably the mark of a merchant—like a 'price tag,' I believe was his phrase."

"I simply suggested," Daley countered, tossing his head and brushing his hair back, "that discovering the medallion on *anything* after the Savonarola fire was highly unlikely."

"And *I* suggested," Vittorio said, addressing Clint McCauley, "that if you would be gracious enough to send us down in your car, this is one disagreement that need not wait until tomorrow to be resolved. It will take only a few minutes to show Signore Daley that the perforations on the painting correspond to those on the official emblem."

"Of course. The limousine is at your disposal," McCauley said.

Vittorio had thrown down the challenge and Daley couldn't refuse. Rosa sat shaking her head, despairing, as she had innumerable times before, of her husband's temper.

McCauley and Andrea exchanged amused glances.

It was agreed that Daley, Vittorio, Rosa, and Andrea would visit the Accademia tonight. McCauley declined to accompany them, saying he could wait until the next morning for the results.

The full moon had a veil across it now—the first threads of a skein of moisture-laden clouds drifting toward the city. Bud McCauley turned off Via deli Alfani onto Via Ricasoli, slowed and stopped in front of the Galleria dell'Accademia. A few fat drops of rain sizzled in the headlights and splattered in the street.

Vittorio bounded out of the car and stood fumbling with the first of two keys required to open the massive front door. His companions followed and stood hunched

66

against the light rain. It would have been simpler to go in through the basement, Andrea thought. But Vittorio obviously wanted to give Tom Daley the grand tour through the exhibition hall.

The door swung open and they went into the dimly lit entrance. Andrea half expected the guard, Luca, to be scrambling to his feet, rubbing the sleep out of his eyes as he usually did each morning when she came in, but he was nowhere to be seen. At the sound of the door, the guard on the second floor came to the top of the staircase, gun drawn. Seeing who was there he quickly retreated, probably to his own favorite spot to nap.

Only a few key lights were left on at night, and the Accademia took on the atmosphere of a mausoleum. Eyes seemed to stare from the paintings, statues and tapestries—indignant at having the silence violated. In the domed apse at the end of the hall the statue of David stood serene and confident. Seeing him, as always Andrea thought of the words of Samuel; *He was ruddy, and withal of beautiful countenance, and goodly to look to.*

They reached the back of the building and the open grillwork elevator next to Vittorio's office. The door clanked noisily as Vittorio slid it open, and they crowded into the small cubicle—the sleepy Rosa Sassetti, still indignant Vittorio, haughty Tom Daley, bored Bud McCauley, and Andrea, whose thoughts were on the Arnoldi miniature in her evening bag—and despite herself, on the man who had given it to her.

There was a lurch, a grinding sound, a short descent, then a jerk of the cable that made them all bend their knees at the sudden stop. The ancient elevator was operating as reluctantly as it usually did.

The basement was dark. There was only the dim bulb above their heads in the elevator. Andrea wondered why the light in the security office wasn't on. Had Luca taken to sleeping in the basement instead of upstairs?

"*Uno momento,*" Vittorio said, sliding the metal door back. He stepped outside and felt along the wall for a switch a few feet away. There was a hum and a momentary flicker as electricity traveled down the fluorescent tubes and locked in its cold bluish light. Then Rosa, standing behind Andrea, gasped.

Andrea turned toward her, wondering what had happened. Seeing the fear on Rosa's face, she knew the trouble was not inside the elevator but back in the basement.

Two men, one on each side of the elevator, stood facing them. Both had silk scarves across their faces. The scarves were knotted under knitted caps so that not even the men's hair was visible, only their eyes. Both held guns.

"Come in," one of them said, "and quietly please. We wouldn't want to disturb the guard upstairs."

Tom Daley stabbed frantically at the elevator button, trying to make it return to the first floor, but it wouldn't budge with the door open.

"Please. Come in," the spokesman said with a slight bow, motioning them out of the elevator.

Behind them, Andrea saw the open safe. The large plastic envelope had been tossed on the floor next to a pile of cotton batting. On a metal work table in the center of the room, lying face up, was the portrait of David.

Where was Luca? Did they have him tied up somewhere? Or—good God, Andrea thought—had they killed him?

"We will ask you to wait in here." The spokesman for the gunmen opened the door to the room where the portable easels were stored. "Put your hands on the tops of your heads," he said patiently, as though instructing children in the rules of a game.

Bud McCauley hesitated, and the more aggressive of the

two men poked him in the ribs to hurry him along. Then the creases at the corners of the thief's eyes bunched themselves into a deep frown. "What is this?" The metal of his gun clanked against the metal of a concealed one that Bud was wearing in a holster under his arm.

"Smith and Wesson—thrity-seven caliber," Bud deadpanned with a coolness that Andrea thought would have done his uncle proud.

The second gunman still had not spoken. Andrea glanced at him. He was tall and thin with a smooth forehead and wide brown eyes that constantly moved around the room and seemed frightened. His gun hand was trembling. Vittorio had turned to look at him, too.

While the older man in the mask was distracted by removing Bud's gun, a series of things seemed to happen all at once. Vittorio made a sudden lunge toward the man with the trembling hand—who saw the action coming and managed to dodge out of the way. At the sound of their shuffling feet, his partner whirled around and leveled his gun at Vittorio's chest. Rosa screamed. The back door burst open and Luca, the guard, stood framed in the doorway with his gun drawn.

In one continuous movement, the man with the creases in the corners of his eyes made another quarter-turn past Vittorio and fired at Luca. With a look of astonishment, Luca clutched his chest and fell to the floor, the upper half of his torso in the basement workroom, his legs stretching out into the alley. The door he had just opened wheezed and swung slowly back, pinning his body between it and the jamb.

"You've killed him!" The younger intruder's voice teetered on the thin edge of hysteria.

"Just put the picture in the bag," the man who had fired said with infinite calm.

"Cristo!"

"Put the picture in the bag!" his partner commanded, only slightly louder.

The young man took the portrait of David from the table and put it into a large canvas carrying case, working quickly, obviously frantic to be away from there.

"Please keep your hands on top of your heads," the other man told the group in a tone that sounded disappointed that they were not better at following instructions. "All but you, signorina." He grabbed Andrea around the waist and pulled her against him. She felt the barrel of the gun against her neck. "You are coming with us . . . in case someone tries to follow."

Andrea knew it was useless to struggle.

"Now take the painting out to the car and get the engine started," he said to the man holding the canvas bag.

The younger man hurried toward the back door.

"Drag him in here before you leave," the older man said, gesturing toward Luca's body.

The younger man leaned the canvas bag against the wall. Then gasping, sucking in great mouthfuls of air, he pulled the guard's body inside the door, the face scraping against the rough concrete floor. A zigzag trail of blood from the bullet hole in his chest followed Luca. As soon as the body cleared the door, the younger man grabbed the canvas bag and left. Seconds later, there was a retching sound of vomiting outside.

Stumbling footsteps faded in the alley, and a few minutes later the sound of an idling car engine was heard in the parking lot. "Into the storage room, please," the older intruder said to Rosa, Vittorio, Tom, and Bud. They did as he said. "And pull the door closed behind you," he said. Again, they complied.

Andrea glanced at, then away from, Luca's body. He is going to kill me, too, she thought with detached clarity.

As soon as we're away from here, he'll kill me. If there is any chance of getting away, it would have to be now.

Desperately she searched the room for an escape or a weapon. The man, still clutching her at the waist, pulled her toward the door. As she backed along the worktable, she spotted a large pair of shears in a box of paint tubes and chemicals. Suddenly, with all her strength she hit backwards with her fist at the gun at her neck. But the gun didn't fall as it was supposed to; the man's arm merely straightened out.

The scene had the timing of a trapeze act—she twisting away, he grabbing her wrist the split second after she reached across the table—not close enough for the scissors. But as he pulled her away, she managed to scoop up a small plastic packet of powdered sodium hydroxide. The caustic soda used for removing organic deposits from porcelain and stoneware was not the weapon she had hoped for, but the gunman had not seen her take it, and it was small enough to conceal in her fist.

Holding both her wrists behind her with one huge hand, the man now pushed her ahead of him into the alley. Outside the door, they skirted around the bicycle rack where Luca's yellow Vespa, splattered with vomit, was chained.

"Get in the middle," the gunman said when they reached the car, pushing her roughly into the front seat. "And you," he said to the man behind the wheel, "get on the other side. I'll drive."

The younger man came around the front of the car. He had taken the scarf off and was wiping his mouth with it. "You said no one would get hurt."

"Shut up."

The car was already in motion before the man who had been sick got both his legs in and closed the door. It lurched out of the alley and onto Via Ricasoli. Traffic was light at

71

this time of night, and the car skidded through the wet streets unimpeded.

Near the edge of the city, they crossed under the *autostrada* and turned toward the road to Empoli. Andrea drew a map in her mind, recording street names, landmarks. Route 67 was the old hill road through Empoli to Pisa.

It had not been raining when they left, but it was beginning again now. The wet street was a dark mirror of shop windows and neon signs. A truck pulled in front of them from a side street, forcing the car to skid to one side. The gunman slowed, going with the skid, sending a fan-shaped spray of water onto the sidewalk. The car came to a standstill crosswise on the street. The driver cursed and started the ignition again. As he did, he looked at Andrea, then past her at the uncovered face of the man on the other side.

"You idiot," the driver said. For the first time there was anger in his voice. "I *knew* you didn't have any talent, but I thought you at least had some sense."

Andrea didn't know what had made him so angry and turned to judge the other man's reaction. His large eyes looked anguished, his sunken cheeks and pale mouth unhealthy. Beneath the knitted cap pushed back on his head, a cowlick swirled a black curl down on his forehead. He sat with the soiled scarf wadded in his hand. Suddenly she realized why the driver was so upset. The young man's face was uncovered, and she had looked into it. She would be able to identify him!

She glanced at the driver, a reflex action. Their eyes met, and there was recognition on both sides. She had become a danger to the two men.

They drove on in silence, and then the driver said in the same calm voice he'd used in the basement of the Accademia, "You have nothing to be afraid of. As soon as we get out of the city, I'll let you go." She knew he was lying.

Hardly moving her fingers in her lap, she used a thumbnail to remove the staple that held the package of sodium hydroxide closed.

They were approaching an intersection where the traffic light was yellow. The driver looked to the right to see if a car was coming, to make sure he could make it safely through when the light turned red. To the left Andrea saw two men in yellow slickers under an orange neon sign that flashed CAFFÈ EMPOLI. They headed for a car parked at the curb as the man beside her sped through the intersection.

Which hand, Andrea thought, which hand should I put it in? The end of the packet was unfolded now and open. She rehearsed in her mind what she planned to do.

As they left Florence, they turned onto a dirt and gravel road that rose into the Tuscany hills. The younger man with the hollow cheeks was making groaning sounds. "Stop the car," he said.

The driver didn't answer.

It was raining in earnest now. They skidded on the muddy road as rocks hit the underside of the car and the tires crunched and scattered them. The stench of vomit from the younger man's scarf and clothes was almost unbearable in such close quarters.

"I am going to be sick again," he said.

"Press your finger between your nose and upper lip," the driver commanded calmly.

The younger man put his hand over his mouth, muffling the gagging, retching sounds. "No," he said, "I can't hold it back." He began rolling down the window.

They were reaching a curve in the road. On the right side was a steep downward slope held in place by tall grass and a few struggling olive trees. On the left was a high dirt bank that obscured the view around the corner.

Andrea could feel the younger man's body contract as he put his head out the window and began to vomit into the rain.

For a second, the driver's attention was diverted from the road. Andrea took the only chance she was likely to get. With her left hand she grabbed the wheel. With her right, she rubbed the handful of caustic soda into the driver's eyes.

Bellowing in pain, he brought his hands to his face, and tore off his mask. Andrea turned off the ignition and, with both hands on the wheel, jerked the car sharply to a halt against the dirt bank on the opposite side of the road.

The young man, still heaving, opened the door and draped his body across the window. Andrea scrambled on top of him as the driver, with one hand still covering his eyes, grabbed for her in the seat beside him.

The younger man's moaning grew louder as she kicked his shins to move his legs out of the doorway. Falling across his body, she landed face down in the muddy road. On all fours she made for the tall grass on the other side of the road.

The caustic soda would make the gunman's eyes burn for a while, but after a few seconds, when the tears flushed the gritty substance away he'd be able to see. In the time she had, she managed to cross the road and head down the incline. Sliding and stumbling, she took a diagonal path to keep from falling headfirst down the steep hill. Suddenly there was a sharp crack overhead as a bullet ripped off a branch of an olive tree and dropped it in front of her. She fell to the ground, crawling in the deep grass toward a large rock a few yards below. Looking back at the car, she saw her pursuer cross in front of the headlights, wiping his eyes with the scarf, heading in her direction.

Lie still, she thought. No motion. No noise. A shower of mud and rocks hit the back of her legs. The man's heavy

74

shoes tore away at the hill as he started straight down toward her.

A few miles below on the road they had just left, she saw the headlights of a car, hazy yellow in the rain, weaving back and forth on the tangled ribbon of road. Then there was a third light—a red one above the other two—and the almost imperceptible sound of a siren that grew louder as the lights grew larger.

The footsteps above her stopped, then started in the opposite direction, picking up speed crossing the road.

Andrea cautiously peered through the grass as the gunman pushed his partner into the car and slammed the door behind him, then jumped in on the other side. He quickly backed the car away from the embankment and skidded recklessly around the curve of the muddy road as the siren grew still louder and more piercing.

Andrea crawled to the nearest tree and grabbed a low-hanging limb, pulling herself up on shaky legs. She climbed the side of the hill, slipping back once against the jagged edge of a protruding rock. Climbing again, at last she stood in the middle of the road. Frantically, she waved her arms at the approaching headlights. As the car slowed in front of her, she could see blood dripping from the fingers of her right hand.

The police car shut off its siren and stopped in front of her. She stood shivering as the mud that clung to her hair and clothing mixed with the cold rain to become sticky rivulets that streamed down her face, her arms, and her legs.

The green chiffon dress that had looked so stunning earlier in the evening clung to her body like soggy tissue paper. The green velvet jacket, soaked and stained, had one sleeve torn loose at the shoulder. Her shoes had mired in the mud, and she had walked out of them on the climb back up the hill. The cut on her arm throbbed and she had a deep bruise on her left thigh. While she had stood helpless, a painting had been stolen—and a young man had lost his life. And as the two policemen in their yellow slickers got out of the car and came toward her, she almost cried—thinking how lucky she was.

Chapter 9

At the police station Andrea was led past the front desk to the same office she had visited before with the name CAPTAIN ALDO BALZANI written on the door.

"This is the signorina . . ." the uniformed officer who had driven the patrol car began.

"Miss Perkins and I have met," Captain Balzani said. "And Signore Sassetti called to tell us what happened at the Accademia. You had better call him, sergeant, and tell him the signorina is here with us . . . that she's all right. You are, aren't you?" Balzani led Andrea to the same battered-looking chair.

"Yes." She was surprised again by his Southern drawl.

Balzani grinned at her. "You look a little like the winner in a mud-wrestling contest."

Andrea supposed that was an attempt to lighten the situation, but she was not amused. She pushed her dripping hair back from her face. As she did, she noticed there was still blood on her right arm.

"Let me have a look at that," Balzani said, examining the scratch on her shoulder. "Maybe I should call the nurse."

"It's stopped bleeding. I'm fine."

"It seems I'm always prescribing Band Aids for you." Then more seriously, Balzani told her that she could go home if she wanted. That her statement could wait until tomorrow.

"I want to make a statement," she said testily, "and I want to make a complaint."

"What sort of complaint?"

"Those men in the police car that brought me here . . . we could have caught the thieves if they had followed the car, but they refused. They just turned around and came back to the city.'

"No, ma'am. The thieves would have been long gone. They could have turned off on any one of those hill roads at night. But *domani* . . . tomorrow . . ."

Andrea shook her head in exasperation, not understanding the lack of urgency she found everywhere in Italy. "*Domani, domani!* Is everything in this whole country going to happen tomorrow?" She felt like screaming. "You're letting Venice slip into the Adriatic . . . Rome is becoming a garbage heap . . . and now, a guard has been killed and a painting, possibly a masterpiece, has been stolen, and you want to wait until tomorrow to do something about it."

Captain Balzani sat on the corner of his desk, grinning at her. "It's not fair to blame me for Venice and Rome."

"I'm sorry," Andrea said with a sigh, "but I *do* think we could have caught up with those men. But your policemen wouldn't even try."

"They were right not to," Balzani said. "They had you, a civilian, in the car." Then he added, "The men who abducted you were probably on their way to Pisa. We've contacted the police there to be watching for them. Do you think you could identify them?"

"I'm sure I would recognize the younger one, but I only got a glimpse of the driver."

Balzani took two thick photo albums from the top of a filing cabinet and put them on the desk in front of Andrea. Then he left to check the report of the officer who responded to Vittorio Sassetti's frantic call from the Accademia earlier that evening.

For half an hour Andrea searched the expressionless black-and-white glossy faces that stared up from the album at her. The younger thief's picture was not there. But when Balzani returned she had found two other pictures that she could identify.

She pointed to one with the name *Pietro Corsini* beneath it. "This is the man who fired the gun," she said. Yes, that was the face she had seen in the headlights. That was the profile she had seen etched in the darkness on the car window.

Balzani took the picture from the book and went to the door. To an officer outside he gave instructions to have it circulated both in Florence and in Pisa.

"There is another picture I recognized," Andrea said, leafing forward a few pages to the *F*s and pointing at a picture of Leo Fozzi. "That's the manager of the hotel where I live." She was amazed at finding his picture in a police album.

"Oh, yes. We know Leo. He has a nice little black-market operation out of the basement of the Albion."

"Why hasn't he been arrested?"

Balzani explained that he had been, a number of times. But with a little money to the judge—who was a friend of his, and probably a customer—the jail door revolved as easily as the door of the hotel. "We try to keep him on his toes, though. We raid the basement every three or four months."

The police captain flipped through the pages of the report by the investigating officer of the murder and theft at the Accademia. "There was no evidence of a break-in," he said. "The lock on the alley door wasn't damaged. Neither was the one on the safe. How many people have keys?"

"Vittorio Sassetti and I," Andrea replied. "And the guards have keys to the outside doors but not to the safe."

"Does the safe have a combination lock?"

"No. It's called a safe, but actually, it's a small room where objects that are waiting to be catalogued are kept. It has a metal door that is locked with a key."

"So . . . anyone with access to that area of the basement could have taken a wax imprint and had a key made."

"I suppose that's possible."

"Aren't the guards supposed to stay inside the Accademia?"

"Yes."

"But it says here . . . 'The guard came in from the alley and was shot as he entered the basement.' "

That was true, Andrea realized. Why had Luca been outside? And if the door had not been forced, how could the thieves have gotten in without a key?

Oh, God, Andrea thought, Luca must have let them in. He knew the two men were there! Had he gone outside as a lookout, to warn the thieves in case anyone came by? He would not have been expecting someone to come through the front door at that time of night.

"Is the report correct?" Balzani prodded.

"Yes. He came in from the alley," Andrea said.

But if Luca was involved in the robbery, why did Pietro Corsini shoot him? Because he didn't trust Luca? Because he was afraid that if the police questioned the guard he would identify them? After all, the thieves were wearing masks. Luca was the only one who knew who they were.

"Was there only one guard on duty?"

"No, there were two. The upstairs guard spends most of his time on the second floor. The downstairs guard patrols the first floor and the basement."

"Isn't that a big responsibility for just two people?"

"Not really." She explained to him again that everything on display was bolted to the wall or the floor and that the computer also functioned as a burglar alarm system. Everything was wired so that if it was disturbed an alarm sounded at a private security office shared by all the galleries and museums in Florence. But Balzani knew that. And the security office would immediately call the police at any rate. What was he getting at?

"Tell me again why the picture that was stolen didn't set off an alarm?" He tapped his pen on the edge of the desk.

Andrea hesitated an instant, then told him the entire story of the portrait, beginning with the priest from San Miniato and ending with the decision she and Vittorio had made to keep the painting in the basement until it could be catalogued.

Balzani was silent through the entire narrative. When she was finished, he nodded, made a few notes, then asked, "Who was present when the priest gave you the portrait?"

"No one."

"Who examined the portrait other than yourself?"

"No one . . . although Vittorio Sassetti was present." She explained that they had planned to make conclusive tests the next day.

"Do you actually believe it was painted by Michelangelo?"

"Every test we have made so far indicates that it was."

"But it *could* be fake?"

"Yes," Andrea admitted with her usual caution. "It's the right age, the right technique . . . The only thing left to be examined is the signature."

The captain paused, then, "Do you teach at the Accademia?"

"No. Why?"

"I just thought you might have known Gino Corsini."

"Who?"

"Pietro Corsini—the man you identified as the gunman—has a younger brother who is a student at the Accademia. We've been watching Gino for over a year. So far as we know, he's clean. But with his brother's record, we keep an eye on him."

"I told you I had never seen either of them before." Andrea was becoming irritated. Did he think she was lying?

"Tell me how you managed to get out of Pietro's car."

"Wait. I just remembered something. When the man who fired the gun saw that the other one had taken the scarf off his face and that I would be able to identify him, he said, 'I knew you didn't have any talent—but I thought you had some sense.' *Talent* seemed a strange word to use at the time. Do you suppose he meant talent as an artist?"

Balzani shrugged, but made a notation. "Tell me how you got out of Pietro's car," he asked again.

Andrea told him.

"You were pretty lucky, weren't you?"

"What do you mean?"

"Being able to pick up the package of soda without their seeing it, then escaping from two men with guns—and having the police come and scare them off. By the way, at your request, those two policemen were on their way to the Accademia to check around when they saw Pietro Corsini run the red light."

Andrea tensed. She wondered suddenly whether Captain Balzani believed she was involved in some way—that she helped plan the theft—or faked it. "I want to go home," she said.

Balzani looked at her appraisingly. "Yes, I think you have been through quite enough for one day." He went to the door and called to an unseen officer, "Lieutenant, assign someone to watch the hotel where Signorina Perkins lives. And bring a car around." To Andrea he said, "I'll need to question you again later," then he grinned and added, "Sometimes it's better to put things off until *domani.*"

She smiled back at him in spite of herself.

Chapter 10

Above the desk, four TV monitors showed unmoving pictures of the two gates and the two main doors of the villa. On the desk was a push-button telephone that could communicate with several areas on the grounds as well as the outside world. Sitting in the swivel chair, he propped his feet up and studied the toes of his boots, thinking of the fiasco the evening had turned out to be. *Cristo*—everything was falling apart. What exactly had happened? He knew part of what took place at the Accademia, but not all. He pushed the "outside" button on the telephone and dialed. There were two rings, then:

"Albion Hotel."

"Fozzi?"

"*Sì.*"

"What the hell went wrong?"

"It is all right. They got away. The picture is safe."

"Where are they?"

"With relatives in Pisa."

"God. I should have handled the whole thing myself."

"They can be trusted. I have worked with Pietro Corsini for years."

"But the other one . . ."

"It is true that Gino may not have been the best choice."

"You told me they were both experienced."

"They are. It is just that Gino's experience is not with theft but with the Accademia. As a student there he knew the building and where the painting was kept. And the guard was a friend of his."

"That's another thing . . ."

"Unfortunate."

"What about the girl that works at the Accademia?"

"That didn't go quite as planned, either." Fozzi's voice began to waver.

"How exactly *did* it go?"

"They took her with them, but she managed to escape."

"*Merde*." There was a pause, then he continued, "What were they doing there tonight anyway?"

"A simple misunderstanding. The Corsini brothers didn't realize the importance of *when* the painting was to be stolen . . ."

"You got a couple of real idiots, didn't you? They were supposed to take it the night *after* it was authenticated." There was another pause. His voice was threatening when he spoke again. "You'll have to handle the woman, Fozzi."

"What do you mean?"

"I mean no witnesses."

"I'm sure she couldn't identify them. The masks . . ."

"You're not sure of anything!" The man's boots crashed to the floor as he sat forward, spitting his words into the phone. "I know she lives at the Albion. Take care of it."

"But the police are watching the hotel."

"Find a way. And I want that painting tomorrow. I'll call you later and tell you when and where I'll pick it up."

"I'll arrange whatever you say," Fozzi said.

The man reached in his pocket and took out a small metal cylinder—a silencer. "I think you understand how important this is and what will happen if you screw up one more time." He slammed down the phone and twisted the silencer on the barrel of his gun. "Tacrong, carong, craang," he said softly.

Leo Fozzi's hand did not leave the phone when he hung up. He scowled at the receiver, thinking of his caller's fondness for guns.

Fozzi was frightened of the man who had hired him to arrange the theft at the Accademia, but he would not carry out his orders as far as Signorina Andrea Perkins was concerned. After all, how would *he* benefit from her death? Fozzi could buy his way out of prison for almost anything else, but not for murder—not in Italy, where human life was held sacred by everyone except the Mafia and the Red Brigades.

Until now he had limited his criminal activity to the black market, and it paid very well. He never should have gotten involved with the Michelangelo painting. But how could one pass up the opportunity of a lifetime? The signorina was Pietro's problem, not his. He would tell him so. Pietro could deal with it however he pleased.

The phone under Fozzi's hand rang. He jumped as though the sound had been accompanied by an electrical charge. He ran his hand through his sparse hair and picked up the receiver. It was Pietro.

When Pietro Corsini concluded the call he sat watching his brother, Gino.

Look at him, he thought. Even here, even now, he was setting up an easel and taking out his paints. His answer to any problem was to paint. Pietro was no judge of art, but Gino *himself* said that he would never be invited to exhibit his paintings; that he would never be the one that the critics discovered and proclaimed a new genius. He evaluated his ability honestly . . . but still the damned fool painted.

Pietro scratched a bushy eyebrow and thought of what Fozzi had said on the phone. "You have to do something about Signorina Perkins." Fozzi was always brave on the telephone. But face-to-face, Pietro would convince him that he had more opportunities to eliminate her than Pietro did. Pietro smiled to himself. It wasn't hard to frighten Fozzi. And the look of fear he could bring to the eyes of people like Fozzi pleased him. That fool of a guard, Luca, had been too stupid to be frightened. His swaggering and his conspiratorial attitude had always annoyed Pietro. Luca seemed to think he was an equal partner. He had been afraid of the wrong things—his father and having his Vespa taken away.

"*Dio*, poor Luca," Gino sighed, undoubtedly replaying the scene in the basement of the Accademia, but without Pietro's detachment. He stopped the swift strokes of his paintbrush and put his hand to his mouth.

"Paint," Pietro commanded.

Chapter 11

There were two messages in Andrea's mailbox when she got back to the Albion Hotel. The first, from Vittorio, insisted that she must stay with him and Rosa, or at least let Rosa come to stay with her. The second was from Clint McCauley, who suggested she come to stay at the villa. She answered both calls and assured them she was fine and well protected by the police.

After a long shower she fell on the bed. Her body ached from exhaustion, but when her eyes finally closed, sleep was only a light blanket that let the nighttime sounds move across her like a chilly draft. The first rays of morning that sifted through a tear in the blind waked her, and she got up wondering how she could face a day filled with the memories of the one before. As she was dressing the telephone rang.

"*Cara*, you are feeling better?" Vittorio asked.

"Yes."

Again he expressed his concern and wondered what he could do to help. There was nothing, she told him.

"Then perhaps you would help me," Vittorio said.

"Of course. What can I do?"

He told her that Tom Daley had decided to leave today. With the portrait gone, there seemed no reason for him to stay longer.

The thought of the missing painting, the beautiful portrait of David, stabbed at her like the memory of a death after the first defenses have crumbled and the loss becomes a reality.

"His plane leaves this evening," Vittorio continued. He would be leaving from Pisa, as there was no international airport in Florence.

Vittorio explained that at McCauley's villa the evening before, Daley had expressed an interest in the walled-in Camposanto in Pisa, a unique, cloister-like, thirteenth-century cemetery remarkable for its frescoes. Vittorio had offered to accompany him there sometime. "It seems today will be the only opportunity," Vittorio told Andrea. "Disagreeable as I find the man, he did come here at our request, and I feel I should compensate him in some way. The problem is, his Italian is so poor . . . and so that I know you are safe . . . why don't you come with us and act as interpreter?"

Why not? she thought. Anything to keep busy, to block out yesterday's images. "Of course I will. I'll meet you at the Accademia."

Bud McCauley was wearing his usual jeans and Stetson hat with the turkey-feather band when he pulled the limousine to a stop and jumped out to open the door for Andrea and Vittorio.

Tom Daley and Vittorio exchanged minimal greetings.

The trip was only fifty-five miles by *autostrada* and the powerful limousine made it easily in under an hour, but it seemed much longer. There was no conversation at all at first, then Daley launched into his favorite subject, the book he planned to write discrediting the Michelangelo frescoes in the Sistine Chapel.

His inspiration, he told them, had come from the fact that Michelangelo had forged some ancient drawings to fool his painting teacher, Ghirlandaio, and that the young student had actually made and sold fake antiques in Rome. Though it was perfectly true, Andrea knew this was not a part of the artist's life that Vittorio cared to be reminded of. His face was becoming red as it had the night before, and she knew it would take only another phrase or two from Daley to set him off again.

Thankfully, they had reached Via Cattaneo and Pisa's ancient gate of Santa Maria was before them. They passed through and a short distance ahead was the "Meadow of Miracles", containing the magnificent Baptistry, the Camposanto, the Cathedral, and the Bell Tower. The structures stood majestically on a flat green expanse, unadorned by shrubbery, flowers, or trees—as though, for once, nature bowed to the beauty man could create. The tower, leaning a seemingly perilous fourteen feet beyond the natural perpendicular, looked as fragile as if it had been shaped on a beach from surf-swept sand and precariously transplanted to the meadow.

Bud turned the limousine into the parking lot nearest the meadow. Vittorio was first out and stalked toward the crowded sidewalk, motioning Andrea and Daley to follow. Tourists clustered on the walkway in front of the vendors' stands—flimsy wooden frames covered with canvas. Packages of photographic slides were attached by clothespins to the overhang and on shelves and counters were cheap plastic clocks and cups, sun visors, lamps, and key chains—all bearing a decal of the Leaning Tower. The smell of sausages, coffee, popcorn, and cotton candy mingled pleasantly in the soft air.

"This way," Vittorio said, taking Andrea's arm and looking back to make sure Daley had not gotten lost in the crowd. They stepped off the curb where the sidewalk was blocked by a vendor demonstrating a wind-up toy rabbit that hopped twice, sat on its haunches—its head making a complete revolution—then hopped onto the scuffed sneaker of a giggling little boy.

Andrea was sorry to leave the gaiety of the sidewalk for the solemnity of the Camposanto, but Vittorio had already started across the green meadow in that direction.

Pietro Corsini had been waiting in the parking lot in Pisa for a quarter of an hour when he saw the limousine drive in. He had not minded waiting. He had learned patience as a child when he and Gino had spent hours sitting on a bench outside the kitchen door of a restaurant, waiting for their mother to finish her evening shift as a pastry cook.

With nothing else to do, he had watched the cats that prowled the alleys. They would sit motionless, poised, becoming invisible to the rats that frantically scurried through the garbage in the alley. Always, one of the rats would come close enough for the cat's measured pounce.

Gino drew pictures on the backs of discarded menus. Pietro watched the cats.

As a teenager he had copied the cat's technique in the crowded Straw Market. He had learned that if he waited for the right opportunity he could snatch a purse or a billfold without ever being detected.

Now, he sat slouched down in the old four-door Fiat he had borrowed from his uncle (his own car would unquestionably be recognized by the police). The canvas carrying case he had brought with him was hidden under a blanket in the back seat. Pietro rubbed his eyes. They still burned from the powder the signorina had rubbed in them the night before, and his anger began to mount as he thought of the incident. If Fozzi was too cowardly to eliminate her, then Pietro would handle it himself. He could wait. But first, there was the matter of payment for the portrait.

The sound of the vendors hawking souvenirs and the shouts of exuberant youngsters was a constant blur of noise in the background. Finally, Pietro heard the sound

91

he had been waiting for—the click of heel taps of a pair of heavy boots coming toward him.

The man looked as Fozzi had described him. He was tall and slim, like an American cowboy, wearing blue jeans and a wide leather belt with a silver buckle and shiny black lizard cowboy boots.

Pietro got out of the car and stood beside it. The man stopped in front of him. They appraised each other calmly.

"Pietro Corsini?"

Pietro nodded. "Bud McCauley?"

"Yes," Bud said. "Where's the portrait."

Chapter 12

Pietro Corsini took time to light a cigarette and exhale before answering Bud McCauley. "We have something to discuss before I hand the picture over to you."

"What?" Bud glanced around the empty parking lot to make sure they were not being observed.

"My brother and I are going to have to leave the country now."

"So?"

"We had not planned on that. It will be expensive."

"That has nothing to do with me."

"You can understand. Murder was never a part of the agreement. But since I had to shoot the guard—and with the police looking for us . . ."

"We agreed on a price," Bud said, his mouth tight with anger. He did not mention that it was Corsini's own fault that he got caught; nor that if he had stolen the painting the night after it was authenticated, as he was supposed to, there probably would have been no problem. But he had not come here to argue. He waited for Pietro Corsini's next move.

Pietro leaned against the car without speaking until his cigarette was half gone. Thoughtfully he scratched his eyebrow and said, "That is true, we did agree on a price. But Fozzi has contacts with art collectors in Rome who might think it is worth more than the amount we quoted you . . ."

A couple with a young boy walked past. The boy was holding a balloon that escaped his grip and floated toward the two men, drifting into the side of the car and falling at Bud's feet. Bud picked it up and handed it back to the child, acknowledged the parents' thanks and watched as they let down the tailgate of their station wagon and spread a picnic lunch.

"How much?" Bud asked, reaching inside his denim jacket and caressing his gun.

Pietro named a price half again as much as the original.

"All right," Bud said. He was good at waiting, too. "Bring it over and put it in the trunk of the limo."

The little boy, with the string of the balloon now tied securely around his wrist, waved as Bud went past followed by Pietro carrying a large canvas bag.

Vittorio's guided tour of the Camposanto—the Holy Field, or Cemetery—was no more successful than the drive to Pisa had been.

Andrea, Tom Daley, and Vittorio had walked down one of the four corridors surrounding a large square filled with earth that had been brought back from the Holy Land by the Crusaders, and past a large collection of Greek, Roman, and Etruscan sculptures. Vittorio stopped in front of an immense wall painting of Christ being held aloft by the Apostles. "The third Apostle here," Vittorio said, pointing to a face strangely different from the others, "is actually a self-portrait of the artist."

Daley gave the life-sized face a brief examination, sniffed, tossed his head back in boredom, then pointed to the upper edge of the fresco where gray-green fungus flowerettes were beginning to spread. "Another case of the Italian creeping crud, I see," he said.

Andrea agreed that the decay that was attacking and destroying so much of Italy's religious art was something to be noted, and if possible, corrected. But Daley insisted on looking at the worm and not at the apple. She could see that her ability as a translator was not needed; indeed, if she had translated what either of them said verbatim, one—probably Daley—would have ended up with a bloody nose. After a while, she pleaded fatigue and excused herself. "I'll wait for you in the limousine," she said in response to Vittorio's sympathetic pat on the shoulder and Daley's arched eyebrows.

Outside, she was alone for a few moments as she cut across the wide meadow. Then two policemen eating candy apples came toward her, smiling, nodding, turning to look appreciatively as she passed them. When she reached the sidewalk she had to contend with the crowd again. Keeping her head down, she gently pushed her way through to the entrance of the parking lot. She looked up then to get her bearings and locate the limousine. It was at the opposite end, near the white booth occupied by the parking attendant. Andrea saw Bud McCauley closing and locking the trunk as another man crossed behind the automobile and went around the corner of the small white building. Her eyes met the man's, and each recognized the other instantly.

Pietro Corsini was the first to react. He smiled.

Andrea turned quickly back toward the sidewalk. Get into the crowd, she thought. That seemed the only hope. He would not hesitate to kill her. She knew that. Even here. Shoving in front of a family group leaving the parking lot, she hurried toward the vendors' stalls. Her eyes searched desperately for the policemen she had seen earlier. Where were they? She looked back and saw Pietro towering above four sleek-haired Japanese girls. He pushed through the group and left them chattering angrily behind him, like a quartet from *The Mikado*. Then suddenly with one feline movement Pietro's arm shot out and a strong hand grabbed her elbow from behind. "*Mia moglie*," Pietro said, smiling at the crowd that jostled past them in both directions. My wife.

"If you scream," Pietro Corsini said to Andrea, "I will say you have run away and I have come to take you home." He shoved her roughly back toward the parking lot.

For a moment she was too frightened to scream. Then she made a piercing cry, at first for help, and then in horror at what had happened to Pietro's face.

He made a sound that was not a word—a harsh, heavy exhaling—and a convex red circle appeared on his forehead at the same instant something wet splashed against Andrea's face and on her hair.

Pietro's hand fell away from her arm and he dropped to his knees. And as a stunned group of tourists stepped back and looked down at him, his body pitched forward on the sidewalk.

Andrea pressed both her hands against her mouth to stop the scream. For a moment nothing moved. Then, beside Pietro Corsini's lifeless body, a toy rabbit hopped twice, sat up on its haunches and turned its head all the way around.

No one saw Bud McCauley step back behind one of the vendors' stalls. No one saw him drop the gun with the silencer into his pocket.

He felt revived and rejuvenated. He had settled another matter of honor.

The terms for stealing the portrait of David had been agreed upon, and Pietro Corsini had changed them. Bud stuck a thumb in his waistband on either side of the silver buckle. "Tacrong, carong, craang," he said.

Chapter 13

The magnet of disaster drew people from all over the Meadow of Miracles. Some still wore the remnants of a holiday smile until they saw why the crowd had collected.

The two policemen had shoved their way through and were asking bystanders, "Do you know who that man is? Did you see what happened?"

"His name is Pietro Corsini, but I don't know what happened," Andrea said.

Her body had seemed to go slack. She might have crumpled had Vittorio not appeared and taken her arm. He, with Daley at his side, began to question her along with the police.

One of the policemen went to call for an ambulance. The other said to Andrea, "You'll have to come to the station with us, signorina. We will have to take your statement."

"I will go with you, *cara*," Vittorio said, putting his arm protectively around her.

"No. I'm all right."

Daley looked at his watch and grudgingly said, "There's plenty of time. If need be I can take a cab from the police station to the airport."

"It isn't necessary," Andrea said. "The two of you go ahead and have dinner as we planned."

Watching them impatiently, the policeman asked if she were ready to go.

"Yes, of course," she said, walking with him to the car parked at the curb.

"I will telephone you from the airport," Vittorio called after her, the concern in his voice resonating against the protective shell she was trying to pull around her. Under his sympathetic gaze and with his shoulder to lean on, her shivering might have turned to sobbing. It was better to be alone with the unknown policeman. She was not as likely to lose control in front of strangers.

The Pisa police station was much like the one in Florence. The narrow hallway was flanked by bulletin boards posted with copies of regulations whose pages had long since yellowed and curled at the edges. Andrea was shown into a large room on the left. At the far end of the office was a long table stacked with books of photographs of known criminals; the same sort she had seen in Florence. A muscular dark-haired man was bent over one of the books and did not look up when she entered.

"If you will sit there, Signorina Perkins . . ." A short, balding policeman whose stomach hung over a worn belt gestured to a chair next to a desk with a disordered stack of papers on it.

The man at the long table looked up at the mention of her name. "Miss Perkins," he said. Andrea turned and was surprised to see Captain Balzani from Florence. "Are you making a tour of Tuscan police stations?" His American Southern drawl was reassuring in these surroundings.

"Not by choice," she answered.

Balzani drew the officer who had driven her to the station aside and they talked quietly together for several minutes. Then Balzani pulled up a chair and straddled it, listening to Andrea, watching her as the Pisa policeman began his questions.

No, she had not seen who shot Pietro Corsini. Yes, he was the same man who had abducted her the night before. Yes, he was gripping her arm when he was hit by the bullet.

After the third time through the same list of questions, the policeman looked at Balzani, and with upturned palms and a shrug of the shoulders, dismissed Andrea.

"I told him you would be willing to talk with them again if necessary," Balzani said, returning to the long table at the end of the room and picking up his briefcase. "I've finished what I was doing here. I'll take you back to Florence."

Andrea knew it would be some time before Vittorio returned from the airport, and though she did not particularly relish the thought of Balzani's company, the idea of waiting at the police station was even less appealing. "I'll have to leave a message at the desk for Signore Sassetti," she said.

The police car did not ride as smoothly as the limousine, and Andrea assumed that Balzani would desert the rough dirt and blacktop road for the smooth, wide *autostrada*. But when they reached Route 12, he turned instead toward the marina.

"A couple of my men are checking out fishing boats," Balzani said. "I want to touch base with them before we leave. Some of the Corsinis are fishermen. They may know where Pietro and Gino were staying."

As they were approaching the Solferino Bridge, Balzani unhooked the microphone that hung beneath the police radio. He pressed the button on the mouthpiece, and the static that had seemed constant cleared as he instructed his men to meet him near the church of Santa Maria della Spina.

Under other circumstances the visit to the marina would have been very pleasant. The fishing boats bobbed in the water and the masts moved up and down as though they were attached to a lazy system of pistons. A red sun hung low over the Ligurian Sea. A few boats, their white sails filled with the light breeze, glided out toward the sun but tacked back to the shoreline like children only wanting to get their toes wet.

Balzani parked and left the car. Two men wearing dark-colored, heavy jackets and knitted caps came to meet him. They stood together, talking.

Andrea gazed out the window at the small church nearby. It had been built in the fourteenth century for sailors about to go to sea, and could be reached only by boat. It rose out of the water as though it had been constructed on the ocean floor and floated to the top.

When Balzani returned, he backed the car out of the parking area of the marina and headed at last for the *autostrada*.

They talked a bit of the beauty of the countryside, and then Balzani's voice changed and he asked Andrea a direct question. "You're sure you saw no one—no one with a gun who could have shot Pietro Corsini?"

Yes, she was sure.

Then he asked, "Since we know he had the portrait, can you think of anyone who might not want it found?"

This surprised her. Who would not want it found? No one who stole it would want it found. Then something else occurred to her. If someone knew that it was *not* a genuine painting by Michelangelo, he would not want it examined. But who would have that knowledge? Only she and Vittorio had tested it. My God, she thought, as a chill ran through her, does Balzani think I invented the whole thing just for publicity? To, in some obscure way, further my career? If he thinks that, farfetched as it might be, he might even believe that *I* killed Pietro Corsini.

Of course, Balzani had not actually accused her, but his

questions frightened her and made her defensive—which, she knew, added another layer of guilt, as far as he was concerned.

The irritating police radio stopped its crackling for a moment and a clear voice came through. "Captain Balzani?"

Balzani picked up the speaker and answered into it.

"We searched the uncle's boat," the caller said. "Gino was not there. Naturally, the uncle has no idea where he is."

"Naturally. Keep after it. Check all the cousins, second cousins, uncles . . ."

"We did find something."

"Yeah?"

"We found the picture."

Chapter 14

Andrea and Vittorio already had the Mc36 set up when Tom Daley arrived at the Accademia the next morning, complaining about the inconvenience of having to return to Florence just as he was about to board the plane back to Texas.

Captain Balzani had persuaded the Pisa police to release the portrait of David to him with a "Special Circumstances" receipt. He had personally delivered the painting to the Accademia, and without an invitation stayed to watch the examination.

Daley busied himself rechecking the jumble of electrical cables that led from the X-ray room to the computer as Andrea carried the portrait inside the cubicle to place it on the metal rack. She secured the upper corners, then slid her fingers down the smooth sides to lock it in at the bottom. Something was wrong. A heart-stopping instinct told her that something was very wrong.

"Vittorio," she said, trying to sound as natural as possible, "would you come in here for a moment?"

Catching the unfamiliar register of her voice, Vittorio hurried to join her. "Yes, *cara*?" He let the door to the small X-ray room glide shut behind him.

"Are you sure this is the same portrait Captain Balzani brought to you this morning?"

"Of course. Is it damaged?" he asked anxiously.

"No, it's in excellent condition . . ."

"Then what . . ."

"Nothing, nothing . . . let's go on with the test."

But there *was* something. She needed a moment to think. Vittorio looked at her quizzically and went back to join Daley.

This was not the portrait the priest had given her.

The moment she ran her fingers down the side of the stretcher, she had realized it. The canvas that was secured around the edges was clean. The painting she had examined before had glue smudges—smudges left years ago when the canvas was cut from the original stretcher and glued to a newer, stronger one.

The thieves could have cleaned the glue away—but why? No, she thought as she studied the edges of the portrait more closely, running her finger down the side, flicking it with her fingernail. No—there was only one canvas here.

This was not the portrait the priest had given her.

How could that be? It had only been away from the Accademia for two days. Even if there had been time to make a copy of the original (and some copyists worked amazingly fast) there would not have been time for it to dry. Even acrylic paint would take two and a half days, and oil paint could take fifty years or more to dry completely. Could the copy have been made years ago? Had someone in the priest's family realized the portrait's value and copied the original? That was possible, but why would the copy turn up now?

Then Andrea realized that there was one way it could have been done. Whoever made the copy probably had a supply of canvases from the era of Michelangelo. Bad paintings from the 1400s were prized only slightly higher by the Florentines than bad contemporary paintings. The copyist had probably scraped the top layers of pigment off—down to the white undercoating—then reproduced the portrait of David on top of it. She had no choice. She had to tell Daley and Vittorio—and Captain Balzani—that it was a fake.

She forced herself to leave the safety of the X-ray cubicle and went back into the workroom where Daley had already begun examining a core sample—a minute layer-cake-like sampling taken from the canvas by the hollow needle of a probe.

"Incredible . . ." Daley said, looking at the printed information that was beginning to accumulate. He spoke with more animation in his voice than Andrea had ever heard before.

"Please turn the computer off a moment," she said quietly.

"This is beyond belief," Daley said, not looking up. "It's actually checking out."

Vittorio stood looking over Daley's shoulder, muttering enthusiastically, hardly able to control his excitement.

"Turn the damned thing off!" she said loudly.

"Have you come unhinged?" Daley turned off the Mc36. "Look," he said, thrusting the computer printout at her. The wood from the stretcher was . . . 1451. The canvas? The same. The white undercoating? The same. The computer's analyzer worked from the bottom up, and had not yet identified the pigment.

"That portrait will not pass the signature pressure analysis," Andrea said. "And when you see the results on the pigment it will contain formaldehyde resin."

Daley, Vittorio, and Balzani stared at her, unbelieving.

"This is not the portrait the priest gave to me."

Formaldehyde resin was the only medium that would permit the forgery to be made in so short a time, she had realized. The pigment had been suspended in a formaldehyde resin that would dry quickly and, for added insurance, the canvas had probably spent several hours in the slow oven of someone's kitchen range.

No one spoke, but Daley turned the computer on again.

A dozen digits and two red warning lights later, the Mc36 printed out: PIGMENT SUSPENDED IN FORMALDEHYDE RESIN.

With the computer still clicking out the truth, Andrea left the basement workroom of the Accademia. She grabbed her jacket and shoulder bag and walked out the heavy metal door, up the alley to the corner, and turned left. There was no point in standing and staring into the questioning faces of Vittorio, Daley, and Balzani. She had no answers. All she could think to do was to walk . . . to move.

As she got farther and farther from the Accademia, her internal compass began to spin crazily. Her usually accurate sense of direction was out of whack. But it didn't matter, the important thing was to be moving.

At the corner of Via del Campidoglio a red light kept her from crossing the street, but it did not stop her. Like a jogger not wanting to break stride, she walked back from the curb to the doorway of a corner auto parts store three times, counting four steps each way, until the light was green and she could cross. Andrea had learned the city of Florence by taking long walks, and she had practiced her Italian by translating the street signs. They all had their own story. Via del Campidoglio—Street of the Capitol. A temple of Jupiter had once stood there.

As she reached the opposite curb a young man on a Vespa yelled something at her and waved as he swerved in front of a bus and disappeared in the traffic. She thought of Luca's pathetic yellow Vespa splattered with vomit in the alley behind the Accademia. No, she told herself, don't think about that.

Via del Sapponai—Street of the Soapmakers. There were no soapmakers now. There was a furniture store, a pizza parlor, and a souvenir shop.

It had been David's face. The eyes were the same fathomless blue. There was the same straight nose and strong neck and shoulders. But there was no question that the portrait was a fake. It was the best fake she had ever seen. Strange, Andrea thought, the difference between genius and craftsmanship. How one person could conceive and execute a work of art . . . and another could direct his hands to copy it so exactly. How did that sonnet go?

> ——— *Creative Art*
> *Whether the instrument of words she use*
> *Or pencil pregnant with ethereal hues*
> *Demands the service of a mind and heart,*
> *Though sensitive yet in their weakest part,*
> *Heroically fashioned.*

Wordsworth? No. Shakespeare? Who could have painted the portrait? Luca could have. Vittorio said he was as talented as any student he had ever seen but was lazy—only interested in flirting with the models and riding his Vespa. But Luca had been shot before the portrait ever left the Accademia. His body had fallen face down on the concrete floor, wedged in the doorway, his feet in the alley. No!

Via della Terme—Street of the Baths. The Romans had built sumptuous baths which now had been replaced by a record store, a candy shop, and a leather-goods store.

The portrait could have passed carbon dating. It could even have been verified by X ray. But the Mc36 was infallible, especially in its examination of signatures. It

106

could determine the pressure, fluidity, and length of each stroke. A signature could not be duplicated.

Could the forged David have been painted by Pietro Corsini's brother, Gino? Captain Balzani had said he was a student at the Accademia, too. Gino had been as frightened as she was as his brother drove them recklessly up through the Tuscan hills, the portrait of David in the canvas bag in the back, banging against the seat at every curve, and the stench in the closed car . . . the smell of Gino's vomit on his shirt . . .

She read aloud: Via dei Calzaiuoli—Street of the Stockingmakers. It was still *the* street for buying shoes. Andrea was momentarily diverted by the plush show-rooms and the elegant displays of footwear.

What was Balzani doing at the Accademia this morn-ing? Was it curiosity or was there some police reason for determining if the portrait was genuine? He sat silently, listening as Daley held forth in his smug, patronizing way. "One could hardly resist the romanticism of it all . . . I mean, a mysterious priest . . . and uncovering the portrait in the hallowed halls where the statue of David stands . . ." Did Daley believe that she was simply inept as a restorer? Or did he believe, as Captain Balzani seemed to, that she had planned the whole fiasco herself? It didn't matter what Daley thought—or that Southern-fried *poliziotto*, either.

Ponte Vecchio—Old Bridge. It was certainly that. It had linked the two banks of the Arno for almost seven hundred years. Andrea entered the covered passageway that had been built so that Grand Duke Cosimo de' Medici could go from the Pitti Palace to the Uffizi without getting wet. Automobiles were not permitted on the bridge. The only vehicles she saw were a baby perambulator and the bicycles of three teenagers who rested on them in the center of the cobblestone walkway. One of the three was a girl with long brown hair that hid her face in profile except for the tip of her nose as she bent forward playing a wooden flute she'd purchased at the Straw Market. Andrea walked around them, joining the throng of shoppers. The dissonant sound of the flute gave the afternoon air a medieval feel.

The crowd was thick and slow-moving. Andrea, not wanting to change her pace, turned to retrace her steps. She almost tripped over a frail little lady in a wheelchair being pushed by a robust younger woman. When she reached the street and turned toward her hotel, she felt a strange absence. What was missing? What had she lost? Guilt—that was it. For the first time since she was a small child, she had seen a wheelchair and had felt no guilt. She regarded the woman who could not walk exactly as she did the other shoppers. Who could tell what was hidden under the vacation hats, the madras shirts, and blue jeans—what ulcers, cancers, damaged hearts, even mangled brains? Or which perfect specimen would step in front of a speeding truck or be the victim of a knife or bullet? And Andrea could help none of them, nor was she responsible for anyone else's pain. She had not caused her sister to spend her life with a lap rug across her knees. And she had not banished McCauley's wife to Palm Beach where she never rose to greet her guests.

In the crucible of the last two days of her own life, Andrea's view of mortality had changed. She had seen two men die—Luca, the guard, strong, young, barely past his teens, and Pietro Corsini, with strength and agility, at the peak of manhood. It wasn't the blood or the sound of the gun or even the grotesque sprawl of their bodies that would never leave her memory; it was the eyes . . . eyes that had reflected the light of crystallized emotion and had, in an instant, become as opaque as marble.

Andrea crossed to the sidewalk that paralleled the river.

She listened to the hum and splash of the moving water, and breathed in the dampness that smelled of underwater vegetation, and touched her tongue to the spray that tasted of fish. Leaning over the stone wall, she reached her hands out toward it to feel the moisture. She wanted all her senses to be melded to the moment. Until two days ago the sinew of her life had seemed impervious even to attrition, but twice that sinew had nearly been snapped.

Finally, aware of her tiredness, she crossed the street, walking in the direction of her hotel. Glancing up at the street sign as she turned the corner she read, Via de Macellaio—Street of the Butchers.

Chapter 15

The Albion Hotel's revolving door whooshed softly as Andrea stepped into the lobby unnoticed. A middle-aged American couple from Corvallis, Oregon (they had told Andrea earlier in the week at breakfast), were studying the paintings that covered the walls of the lobby. Their attention was being directed by the proprietor, Leo Fozzi, who looked especially dapper in a deep lavender cravat just two shades lighter than his hair.

He's at it again, Andrea thought absently as she went behind the reception desk to collect her mail and messages.

"What do you think of this one, Vera?" the man from Corvallis asked his wife, pointing to a portrait of a snooty-looking young man in padded taffeta vest with long brocade sleeves with lace at the wrists.

"Oh, signore . . . I am sorry," Fozzi said, putting his short, plump fingers to his forehead, "That is the only one of all my paintings I could not sell."

In Andrea's mailbox was an invitation to the opening of a new gallery and a computerized form letter from an insurance company.

The tourist, to Fozzi's obvious disappointment, had moved on to a contemporary painting. "Since you seem so taken with the Bronzino portrait," Fozzi said, gently leading the husband back to the painting of the young man, "perhaps . . . well, yes," he said, throwing his hands up in despair, "I will have to sell it sometime . . . what with taxes—and you can see for yourself that half the rooms in the hotel are empty. It is just that this is an original painting by the leading Florentine mannerist, done by his hand in the fourteenth century . . ." Fozzi had both the husband and the wife by the arm now. "Much of his work was murals on walls in Careggi and Castello. Unfortunately, everything there has been destroyed . . ."

Andrea turned to go to her room when she noticed a memo pad on the desk with her name on it and the incomplete notation, "Called to remind you . . ."

"But he painted a few portraits, too, for the Medici," Fozzi was saying with a sweeping gesture toward the aristocratic young man in the painting. "This, I have always felt, was his finest." When Andrea interrupted him, he looked at her pleadingly—silently asking her not to louse up his sale. Everything he had said about Bronzino was true, except that the original painting was a part of the Frick Collection in New York City. Andrea had seen a student from the Accademia bring in this rather sloppy copy the previous week.

She shook her head reprovingly but said only, "Was there another message for me?"

"*Sì.*" Fozzi came trotting over to her with a broad smile and a grimace that the Corvallis couple could not see. "Signore Clint McCauley called to remind you of your dinner engagement." He gave her a conspiratorial wink.

Oh, well, Andrea thought, they'll probably get their money's worth in the stories they can tell back home. "Thank you," she said, going toward the stairs, leaving Fozzi to fend for himself with the tourists.

The thought of McCauley was the first pleasant one she had had since she left the Accademia. In her room she dressed and arranged her hair with more care than she had taken since—since the day of her meeting with McCauley in Boston. She chose a silk jersey dress the color of lime sherbet, an understatement that she knew would show her green eyes and coppery hair to their best advantage.

Once she left the city traffic, her little Alfa Romeo was the only intrusion on the nighttime countryside. The only sound was the hum of her car's engine.

Questions still dropped into her mind like pebbles in a pool, radiating out in concentric circles. Who shot Pietro Corsini on the crowded sidewalk in Pisa—and why? Where was the original portrait of David—would it ever be found? Had she given herself permission to express her feelings for McCauley? What were they? Would he care?

Not until she reached the wrought-iron gate with its figure of Neptune did Andrea wonder how she was going to get through. But when the beam of her headlights hit the gate, it opened magically (in response, she supposed, to a closed-circuit TV screen in the garage). The moment the gate closed behind her she felt safe—as though she were entering a sanctuary, a preserve where she would be protected from outside predators.

Bud met her on the steps of the villa and took her car to the garage.

McCauley was waiting for her. "I'm sorry you had to go through that ordeal this morning," he said. "I know how disappointed you must have been that someone managed to make a copy." He lightly took her face in his hands and kissed her cheek. His lips and fingers were cool, soothing, like balm on a burn. And his words were a gift. He believed her. He believed there actually was a portrait of David painted by Michelangelo.

Andrea turned her head, offering him her lips, then kissed him with an enthusiasm that seemed to surprise and delight him. Stepping back, he grinned and said, "Welcome back, Andrea. I wondered where you'd gone when you left Boston."

And though she expected—wanted—to feel his arms around her, he instead took her elbow and guided her toward the *salone*. "Daley's still here," he said. "We'll have to endure his company awhile . . . at least until after dinner."

Seated on one of the twin couches in front of the fireplace, Daley half rose, then settled back. His hands rested on his knees, a silver cigarette holder with a freshly lit cigarette angled toward the floor from his graceful fingers—like a lily, Andrea thought.

"Green is definitely your color," he said to Andrea, then couldn't resist a bitchy appendage, "Of course you know that."

"I haven't told Andrea about your decision," McCauley said. "I thought you might want to give her the news . . ."

There was a flicker of malice in Daley's eyes that he suppressed and replaced with bravado. "It's something I've been considering for some time. I'm going to rejoin the academic world."

It was hard to believe that he had made the decision willingly, Andrea thought. He had always positively preened with the importance of his position at the McCauley Museum.

"I've been invited to head up the Art History Department at Crockett University."

Andrea looked to McCauley for a reaction, but his face was expressionless. When he turned his head to speak to a servant about dinner, Daley fixed her with a look that could have penetrated granite. The fact that McCauley was a heavy contributor to Houston's Crockett University presumably had something to do with Daley's appointment there. But did Daley think *she* was the reason he had been eased out? Momentarily she felt guilty at the excitement thrashing around inside her. And she wondered if he was right.

Daley made some mumbled reference to signing work orders for the museum after dinner and left McCauley and Andrea having espresso on the portico.

The wide porch overlooked the river, and the reflection of a misshapen moon bobbed in an uneven path across to the opposite side, where it was diffused in a pattern of leafy shadows among the olive trees.

At last, McCauley kissed her thoroughly. His hands slid down her arms and around to the small of her back as he drew her to him. The strength of his body against hers seemed to press out the fear and anguish that had been like a physical presence the last two days. Now she was perfectly willing to let her quickening pulse do her thinking for her.

"Wait a minute," McCauley said with a low, delighted laugh that she could feel rumbling in his chest. He led her to a wicker couch and sat, still holding her hand in a way that seemed pleasantly old-fashioned. "Andrea, I've never asked for anything twice in my life."

"You don't have to now."

"I was going to offer you Daley's job even if you had continued to be so . . . mysterious."

She smiled and brought his hand to her lips.

"I wanted to hire you because you're the best," he said. "That fake this morning hasn't changed my opinion of your ability."

"You may be the only one."

"You'll come to Houston with me?"

"Yes."

"No more disappearing?"

"No."

"You'll tell me why you ran away before?"

"Yes . . . sometime."

"You'll have to work harder than Daley did. I want you to be responsible for my private collection, too."

"You have a private collection in Texas?"

"Some is in Houston, some here. Would you like to see it?"

No hurry, Andrea thought as he kissed her again.

Chapter 16

A butler knocked discreetly on the open door, then asked if anything further was required of him as McCauley and Andrea moved out of their embrace.

"Yes. Bring Miss Perkins her coat."

When the servant was gone and before he returned in less than a minute, Andrea said, "Are you sending me home?"

"Hardly," McCauley laughed, helping her into her quilted brocade wrap, "now that I've found you again. But I want you to see the *salone* where my collection is stored."

He took her hand and led her to a corner of the veranda. At the side was a stairway that led down into vine-covered darkness. McCauley touched a wall switch that turned on a light above a door on the lower landing and revealed a trellis of ivy arched over steep stone steps. "I have an elevator in my bedroom that goes down here, but this way is more impressive, and I want you to have the full treatment."

He preceded Andrea and cautioned her to hold the railing. The door at the bottom dated from 1653, when the villa was built, he told her when they reached the landing. It was made of polished oak with ornate brass fittings. "This used to be a wine cellar," McCauley said, taking a set of keys from his pocket, "but I had it converted to a *salone* and had a new cellar dug underneath."

McCauley pulled the door open to reveal . . . another door. This one was metal and fitted around the frame with a layer of rubber so that not a scintilla of light or a particle of dust could get in. When McCauley unlocked and pushed it inward, a rush of cold air hit Andrea's face.

"The temperature in here is kept at fifty-two degrees," he said, turning on a floor lamp that reflected downward in a circle that fell on the plush beige carpet and the arm of a couch of the same shade. "Sit there, please," he added. "The room is arranged to be seen from that spot."

Andrea sat, leaning into the softness of the cushion. She watched as McCauley went to a glass-screened fireplace on the wall next to her and turned on an automatic gas jet beneath a neatly laid pile of wood. The blue tongues of flame licked at the twigs and set them crackling under a log. The added light sketched in the outline of a dozen or so pictures on the long wall ten feet in front of her. Along the opposite wall, she saw pedestals that held undefined statuary.

"The fire isn't for warmth," McCauley said, reaching down and turning her collar up. A sudden flurry of sparks flew up the chimney, but the fire seemed only an illusion, for not the slightest scent of smoke or degree of heat was allowed to escape from the tightly fitted glass enclosure. "The lighting for this room was the most difficult part to work out," McCauley said. "Electricity just didn't seem to do the paintings justice. They need sunlight—or, second best, the glow of firelight—to temper the artificiality."

The *salone* was sparsely furnished. There was only the couch and a small desk with a straight chair that stood near the door.

"I'm not usually given to theatrics," McCauley said as he reached toward a small panel of switches next to the fireplace, "but you're one of only five people who have

117

been in this room, and I want you to see the collection at its best advantage."

"Who were the others?" She couldn't stop herself from asking. She knew she probably wasn't the only woman ever invited to McCauley's villa, but she wondered who else he had shared this room with.

"Former owners of some of the paintings," he said. "Some of them ask to stop by and look at them from time to time."

Then, one by one, he turned on a series of lights suspended from an overhead track, each directed at a different painting and arranged so there was no glare on any area.

The first frame contained a tondo, a circular painting, of Mars and Venus, the famous lovers. They were seated in a shaded arbor that looked down into a valley, across the horizon and through to infinity.

"There, that's you," McCauley said, indicating the slim, supine figure of Venus with wind-ruffled hair spread across the grass. "Her hair is the same color as yours."

"That's an early Botticelli," Andrea said, staring at the goddess. She was too excited to remain seated and jumped up, looking at the painting from several different angles.

"I *believe* it is." McCauley lightly cupped her shoulder with his hand. "It was authenticated in Rome. But I'd like you to check all of them with the Mc36. There will be some restoration necessary, too. This one, for instance," he said, indicating a large painting next to the Botticelli. "This was cut from its wooden frame during the war and spent several years rolled up in an army footlocker. There's a tear at the bottom."

Andrea studied the painting of a haughty-looking angel in sandals and a flowing yellow dress crisscrossed with white ribbons. The signature was that of Filippo Lippi.

"I saw this painting several years ago in Venice," Andrea said, studying the characteristic elongation of the figure of Lippi's angel and the nervous agitation of the color that gave the painting its vitality. "I thought it was a part of the Getty collection."

"It was," McCauley said with no further explanation.

Next was a painting by Bernardino Luini—a portrait of a young girl in a russet cap with an enigmatic expression on her face.

"That looks like the Mona Lisa wearing a hat," Andrea laughed delightedly.

"There is a similarity, isn't there?" McCauley smiled.

"Luini must have painted it when he was studying with Leonardo."

"The dates coincide," McCauley said. "The student had the effrontery to copy almost exactly the master's style."

He had been right about the fire, Andrea thought. The reflection of the flickering flames cast a moving light across the face in the painting that made the curved lips seem about to open and reveal some unimagined secret.

All in all there were fourteen magnificent examples of Renaissance painting. Among them were two by Paolo Uccello, an allegorical battle scene by Domenico Veneziano, and—most impressive, Andrea thought—an anatomical drawing by Leonardo da Vinci of a human embryo, with notations in Leonardo's own handwriting. She could not read it all, but she could make out, ". . . the heart of this child does not beat, and it does not breathe, because it lies continually in water. If it were to breathe, it would drown, and breathing is not necessary because it receives life and is nourished from the life and food of the mother." Above this notation was a bisected drawing of a womb with a fetus curled inside. The umbilical cord attached to the child's navel looped around a foot, disappearing behind its back, then reappearing above the head and attaching to the womb.

"Does that shock you?" McCauley lightly rubbed his hand across her shoulder.

"I think it's magnificent," she said, not understanding his question. "The detail is incredible."

"No, I mean the fact that he made such a drawing at all."

"Of course not. Without even mentioning painting, think what he contributed to architecture . . . anatomy . . . poetry and music. To say nothing of medicine."

"No," McCauley said, taking one of her hands and leading her back to the couch, "that still is not what I mean. To make a drawing that accurate, he would have had to dissect a pregnant woman—which would have been not only criminal but also fairly gruesome."

Andrea frowned. She had no more thought of the origin of the drawing than she would have wondered about the identity of a corpse necessary to make drawings for a medical book. "What are you asking me?" She was still puzzled.

"The age-old question of moral theologians," McCauley replied, obviously having been leading up to exactly this. "Does the end justify the means?"

How was it possible to know where the body of the woman had come from—or whether the fetus had been alive or dead? Leonardo's biographers had stated that he illegally purchased the bodies of indigents—some stated he even stole them—so that he could dissect them to learn the structure of the human body. This to Andrea was forgivable, even necessary for the knowledge he had contributed. "In Leonardo's case, yes, the means were justified. Just because most of the world was tied up in ignorance and superstition was no reason—"

"So you believe in Nietzsche's *Ubermensch* . . . that there are some supermen—for whatever reason . . .

genius . . . a position of power . . . money . . . who can live above the law?"

"Nietzsche thought that passionate man should use his passions in creative activity—and that's exactly what Leonardo did." Andrea stood again, striking a posture she had often used with her art history classes. "Leonardo believed that a painter had to understand *all* forms of nature." She continued her discourse, defending da Vinci's means of acquiring knowledge. In conclusion she quoted Byron's "Conspiracy": "There's not any law exceeds his knowledge; neither is it lawful that he should stoop to any other law."

McCauley laughed and stood, applauding her performance. Andrea thought how ridiculous she must have looked in her stance as an orator, but she bowed grandly and joined him on the couch.

"I love your enthusiasm," he said, patting her hand. "It's a very important commodity, enthusiasm."

"What do you mean?"

"Leonardo's, for instance. Can you imagine the enthusiasm he must have felt for acquiring—no, let's say it bluntly—for stealing a cadaver? Though most people won't admit it, I believe there are few things as exciting as getting away with something illegal or immoral. In any event, picture him with his cadaver—dissecting it—to find out how a human being was strung together. How satisfying that must have been. After that, what value could the cadaver have for him?"

"I'm not following you . . ."

"This room is another example of the same principle. For me it has become a climate-controlled trophy room."

"Trophy room?"

"Yes. My father had one at the ranch. His had antlers on the wall. Mine has paintings."

"Surely you're not comparing the paintings with . . ."

". . . my father's antlers or Leonardo's cadavers? No, but I will say that the greatest pleasure they've given me was in acquiring them. Possessing them is satisfying, but the pleasure of possession doesn't compare to the pleasure of acquisition—the chase, the hunt, if you will. The Luini painting, for instance; I first saw it in the home of an industrialist in Genoa."

McCauley told her of offering a fair—even generous—price, but the industrialist would not part with it for any amount of money because it had been in his wife's family for three centuries. And so McCauley had let the subject drop—or so the man from Genoa thought.

The industrialist, Emilio Rossi, was among other things somewhat of a visionary. Shortly after World War II, on a visit to America he sensed the public's general appetite for the finer things in life. Americans were tired of food stamps and rationed gasoline and shoddy clothing and shoes with cardboard innersoles. They dined out in restaurants, bought big cars and followed the fashion scene as avidly as the baseball standings. They felt they deserved to indulge themselves, and Emilio Rossi had a plan to help them do it.

When he returned to Italy, he consolidated all his assets and began manufacturing fine-quality leather goods. He hired experienced designers and artisans, who would handmake shoes, belts, and handbags. He paid salaries that were barely enough to feed their families, but his workers had no choice but to accept them; for Italy was many years away from *Il boom* of the 1960s. Meanwhile, Rossi's quality products were eagerly ordered by Neiman-Marcus in Dallas and Saks Fifth Avenue in New York.

By far his best American customer was Keesler and Nugent, as exclusive as the other stores—but with thirty-two outlets across the nation. His first shipment sold out in less than a month. Each month his business grew larger until he had approved plans and committed future earnings to build two new factories. And then came the catastrophe. In January, Keesler and Nugent cut its order in half. In February, there was still another cut. In March there was no order at all. Neiman's and Saks continued to stock as much of his merchandise as they could fit on their shelves, but that would hardly compensate for the loss of the thirty-two Keesler and Nugent stores. The bank was demanding payment on his loan. The architect who designed his two new buildings was threatening to sue. His employees, who had recently become unionized, were demanding more money and threatened to strike. Rossi needed the money *then* or he would be ruined.

He placed a desperate call to Keesler and Nugent's president, Norman Keesler, and was told that the store might be able to give him more orders in the future, but for now there was no need for his products. When Rossi asked for details, Keesler was vague and abrupt. And then he hung up.

Rossi wrote that he was coming to America on business and requested a meeting with Keesler and Nugent's board of directors. His request was granted, and an appointment was made. It was at that meeting that he discovered that Clint J. McCauley was the majority stockholder.

The next day a package was delivered to McCauley's villa in Florence. It contained the Luini painting—with no accompanying note or explanation. Within a week, Emilio Rossi had his largest order ever from Keesler and Nugent.

The relationship had continued to be profitable for both Emilio Rossi and Clint McCauley, although they had met only the one time since the original offer for the painting was made . . . and refused.

As the story unfolded, Andrea became increasingly uneasy. "I thought the painting belonged to his wife's side of the family," she said when he had finished.

"An Italian wife understands that whatever she brings to a marriage is at her husband's disposal," McCauley said, dismissing that detail.

The temperature of the room seemed even colder than before to Andrea, though McCauley had told her it was kept at a constant fifty-two degrees. Her teeth were on the verge of chattering.

"The key to business, as to love," McCauley said, "is to find out what the other person really wants—not what he says he wants." He leaned across the couch and kissed Andrea on the cheek.

He seemed not to notice that she did not move toward his kiss—did not move at all, but rather sat silently watching him as he straightened and crossed the room toward a large bronze statue and took something from behind it.

In a darkened corner, McCauley set up an easel and placed a painting on it. It was in an antique gold-leaf frame that gleamed and sparkled by the light from the fireplace. The design was ornate, with dimpled cupids at each corner. At the upper right, a cherub held a ribbon of flowers. The ribbon draped down from a plump little hand and was caught in the upstretched fingers of the cupid below. This angelic creature, with folded wings, handed the garland to the cherub on his left, who, reaching upward, passed the floral ribbon to the fourth cherub. It was a charming, voluptuous design.

When McCauley had placed the easel at the angle he wanted, he adjusted the track light but paused a moment before turning it on. "I think you've seen this before," he said, smiling, as he focused the lamp dead center on the portrait of David.

Chapter 17

The portrait of David glowed in the changing reflection of light from the fireplace. The cherubs on the gold-leaf frame seemed to wink and smile in the moving shadows. But for Andrea the painting had no more substance than a mirage. How could it be here in Clint McCauley's villa?

Shades of cream and pink and tan, mixed magically on the master painter's palette, gave David's skin a texture that looked pliable; and his expression was so lifelike that the young shepherd in the portrait seemed capable of accounting for his whereabouts the last two days himself. How had McCauley been able to find the portrait when the police had not?

"Bud tracked it down," the Texan said, grinning at her confusion as he answered her unasked question.

"Bud . . . your nephew, Bud?" Her voice sounded to her like the invention of a ventriloquist. "But, how . . . ?"

"It took some doing," he said.

"Yes, but how . . . ?" she began again, still strangely reluctant to go past the fact that the painting was standing on an easel five feet in front of her.

"He took delivery of it yesterday in Pisa," McCauley said.

"Yesterday . . . in *Pisa*?" Again her words seemed to come from some outside source. She sat up straighter, her feet neatly pressed together on the floor. Then she combed her fingers through her hair, as though bringing order to her appearance would do the same for her mind.

She searched McCauley's face for an explanation that his words had not yet conveyed. Yesterday? Yesterday seemed as distant as Boston. Yesterday Bud had driven Vittorio, Daley, and herself to Pisa. How had he been able to contact the thief? Why hadn't he told the police? . . . or had he? Then why the fiasco of examining the fake painting at the Accademia? Why, if it was recovered yesterday, did they go through the absurdity of setting up the Mc36 *this morning* to analyze a fake? Did Vittorio know it was here? Did Daley? No, not Vittorio—he had been even more stunned and embarrassed by the results of the computer's analysis than she. And not Daley, either—she'd watched as his resigned anticipation had turned to smug triumph when the painting proved to be a fake.

Suddenly a current of dread coursed through her. She saw the challenge in McCauley's face and knew he had no intention of returning the portrait to the Accademia. He planned to keep it! He meant for it to stay here in his villa.

"Bud was supposed to have taken possession of it *after* it was authenticated at the Accademia," McCauley said matter-of-factly. He sat next to her and took her hand lightly in his. Some primitive instinct told her not to jerk it away, not to show what she was feeling. Some scent of danger immobilized her, sharpening her senses.

"But it doesn't matter that it was acquired too early," he was saying. "Your word alone is good enough for me to believe it's authentic."

Perhaps, she thought. But he owns the Mc36. He can have it authenticated. But by whom? Daley? No, Daley would love to have this information. It would be better than a gilt-edged insurance policy.

He expects me to accept this!

126

"I'm only sorry the world can't know it was you who recognized the work of Michelangelo," he said, giving her hand a squeeze.

Andrea's thoughts swirled and scattered. She pulled out and strung together only the ones that immediately meshed, leaving the others to be sorted later. Bud was supposed to have taken possession of the portrait after it was authenticated. Yes, McCauley would have preferred it that way. It would have given him more pleasure if the discovery of the painting by Michelangelo had been made public . . . more satisfying to have the world know the painting existed, then disappeared.

He expects me to accept all this—to be a conspirator!

She felt degraded—angry—but she kept her voice controlled. "You arranged to have it stolen," she said, having to hear her own words to believe what had happened.

"I arranged to take possession of it," McCauley said. His expression suggested that he had simply completed a purchase from Sotheby's.

The scent of danger still hung in the air but Andrea said, louder this time, "It was stolen!"

"Andrea, you're intelligent, and I think, sensible." He let go of her hand and, leaning back against the side of the couch, looked at her. "From *whom* was it stolen?—if you insist on that word. Was the portrait stolen from you? From the Accademia? By what right did you have it in the first place?"

She looked at him in astonishment, trying to understand his meaning.

"A priest gave it to you. Am I right?"

Andrea nodded almost imperceptibly. She was listening to his words and hearing her own thoughts that leaped at random like the fingers of flame in the glass-enclosed fireplace.

He expects me to accept the fact that the portrait was stolen for him.

Yesterday, Andrea thought. He said it was delivered yesterday in Pisa. So *that's* why Pietro Corsini was in the parking lot!

"You said the priest told you the portrait had been in his family for four or five hundred years," McCauley was saying. "But where did it come from originally?" He looked at her, not expecting an answer. "Last night at dinner, Vittorio told me it was probably taken from the Medici Palace during the Savonarola purge. Wasn't that his conclusion?"

"Yes," she said.

"The theory, as I understand it, is that the portrait was given to the Medici by Michelangelo as a gift of appreciation. So Lorenzo de' Medici is the only rightful owner—and he's hardly in a position to complain. Everyone who has possessed it subsequently was a receiver of stolen goods."

He expects me to accept this.

A sudden vivid image of the theft in the basement of the Accademia detached itself in her brain like a severed hand of flame that lives an instant in midair. The two masked thieves putting the portrait in a canvas bag . . . the sound of the metal door crashing open . . . Luca, the guard, standing in the doorway in the uniform that made him look more like a frightened child in costume than a figure of authority. First, the flash from Pietro Corsini's gun, then the sound—the look of disbelief on Luca's face—the look that slackened and fell away just before his body collapsed face down on the concrete floor.

"Here is where your thinking is faulty," McCauley said. "You can accept that possession of the painting by the priest's family constituted ownership simply because a distant ancestor with a love of art—or more probably, with an eye for making a profit—saved the painting from

Savonarola's bonfire on the palace grounds . . ."

"Two men were killed," she heard herself say.

"How is that relevant?" McCauley asked. "I am not responsible for that. The guard was shot by the thief, Pietro Corsini, and the police don't seem to have any idea who shot Pietro Corsini yesterday."

Andrea's recall was coming in chunks—pried loose from the whole by a word, a phrase. ". . . no idea who shot Pietro Corsini yesterday . . ." She could see the green of the Meadow of Miracles . . . the blur of the crowd that surrounded her on the sidewalk as she walked toward the parking lot . . . *Where was Bud McCauley?* The undiluted malice in Pietro Corsini's eyes as he grabbed her arm and tried to force her to come with him, warning her not to scream. *Where was Bud McCauley?* . . . the hole that suddenly appeared in Pietro's forehead . . . the blood that spurted like carmine pigment . . . that splashed on her cheek and clotted in her hair. *Where was Bud McCauley? Where had the shot come from? Who had fired it? If the thieves had bungled the theft of the portrait . . . if they stole it too soon . . . would that be reason enough? Oh, God. Could Bud McCauley have shot him?*

He expects me to accept the fact that two men are dead.

"Here's my bargain with you," McCauley said, reaching over and touching her hair, smoothing it behind her shoulder. "I'll see that the Accademia gets the portrait of David after my death—everything in this room, for that matter, if that will make you happy." He made a sweeping gesture that included the Botticelli, the Luini, the Leonardo drawing—all the paintings and statuary. "According to insurance actuary tables I have another twenty-five or thirty years." He smiled at her. The white squint lines that had been so charming before now seemed a reptilian protection for the metallic blue eyes that could wait endlessly unblinking until their prey took one step

129

too near.

He thinks I'll accept this.

"In Italy, time is relative," he said. "The portrait has already been lost for five centuries. What difference does thirty years make?"

"You're asking me to accept the fact that . . ."

"I know it's a lot to absorb at one sitting."

"Quite a lot." Dear God, she thought, could she buy some time? Could she ask him to give her time to think about it? But she didn't have to ask.

"Take some time," he said, rising, touching her cheek with the back of his hand. "Think about what I've said."

Andrea, numb, sat watching the erratic dance of the flames. Then she heard a whirring sound and turned to see a door slide open in the wall. McCauley stepped into the small elevator. "I'll leave you alone for a while," he said. "Is fifteen minutes enough?" The door closed, and the elevator efficiently rose to the next level. There was a soft sliding sound as the door opened to his bedroom above, and then silence.

He expects me to share in this.

Then she faced the question that could no longer be avoided. What would happen if she refused?

Could she possibly just say, "No, thank you," and leave? Would he let her go? Hardly—she had seen the portrait here. He had confided his plans. What would he do if she refused to accept his offer? This was a man for whom two deaths were not even an inconvenience. She had better find a way to get the hell out of here!

She looked around the windowless room. There was only the door they had entered from the stairway. She had heard it click when they came in. But was it locked? She hurried to it and tried the handle. It didn't budge.

The only link with the outside was the telephone on the desk. Did she dare try to call the police? She crept toward the desk, studying the phone as though it were some untested instrument she was seeing for the first time. There were several buttons marked KITCHEN, GARAGE, HOUSTON, BEDROOM, DINING ROOM, SALONE I, OUTSIDE. If she pressed the outside button and picked up the receiver, a light would go on. Would McCauley see? Was he upstairs now watching the phone to see if she would use it? She put her hand on the receiver, gripping it but not lifting it from the cradle. Was it worth the chance? She could call Captain Balzani, but it would take him at least twenty minutes—closer to thirty—to get there. *If* he was in. And how much credibility would anyone else at the police station give her story? What did she had to report except that she had found a stolen painting? That was how it was recorded on the police blotter—a painting. At her request, Balzani had made no mention of Michelangelo. Reluctantly she relaxed her grip on the phone. To call would be too dangerous.

On the desk next to the telephone was an antique onyx inkstand, a cube of red wax, a bronze seal (the design of which she did not stop to investigate) and an Etruscan knife with a jeweled handle (used as a letter opener?). She picked up the knife and weighed it in her hand. Could she force the lock with it? She went to the door again. Because of the rubber seal between the door and the frame, the knife slid easily next to the handle where the lock would be. The blade was wafer-thin but made of strong tempered steel. She heard it clink against the bottom of the lock. If she could insert the tip sideways and push back . . .

Following the curve of the lock, she pressed gently against it and felt it give a little. Thank God! She moved the blade up a fraction of an inch and in farther. She could feel the leverage was right. Pushing harder this time, she brought the blade perpendicular to the door. Holding it firmly in place with her left hand, she tried the handle again. This time she was able to twist it and pull it open—and found herself staring at the outer door she had forgotten was there.

"Damn!" she said, all but screaming in her exasperation. She let the first door glide to against her, using her body as a wedge. She tried the same technique on the outer door but with no success. Thin as the blade was, only the tip could penetrate between the ancient oak slab and its sturdy frame. She gave up and leaned against the wall.

Be calm, she thought, closing her eyes, breathing deeply. What other possibilities were there? The elevator! It would have to go down as well as up. There was a wine cellar below, McCauley had said. She'd been able to jimmy the door. If she could get into the cellar, maybe she could find a way out from there.

She hurried to the wall where the elevator was and examined it. Instead of the UP and DOWN buttons she had expected to find, there was a lock. Only a key could activate it.

Dear God, was she running out of time? He had said fifteen minutes.

The knife again; she tried using it to turn the lock. She inserted the tip of the blade into the grooved opening, knowing it was not likely to work. The cylinder turned an eighth of an inch to the left, but no further. Then she felt weak and frightened at what she had almost done. Of course he would hear the elevator. He could be down the outside stairs and waiting for her before she reached the bottom floor—if the elevator went down that far!

Think. She went back to the desk and leaned against it. Maybe she could pretend to accept his offer. Could she convince him? She looked down at her trembling hands. Not very likely, she admitted to herself.

Crossing the room, she stood shivering in front of the fireplace that gave only the illusion of warmth. The largest log was blazing now, reflecting its light on the face of David and sending no heat into the room through its insulated glass doors. You're being crazy, she told herself. If you got out—what then? If she went to the garage and demanded her car, would they open the gate for her without consulting him first?

Then a thought she was not prepared to deal with slithered into her mind. Did she really *want* to escape?

Was what McCauley suggested so terrible? What difference did thirty years make? He said the secret to business—and love—was to find out what people really wanted. Was what she really wanted to be curator of the McCauley Museum—and to share Clint McCauley's bed? Was that what he had counted on? Did he know her better than she knew herself?

Wasn't he offering everything she had always thought she wanted? The recognition—the challenge of the job . . . the attention . . . the stimulation of a handsome, powerful man?

If she accepted his offer, what would be her crime? Strictly one of omission: to do nothing, to tell no one about the portrait of David. Wasn't it enough to know that it was safe?

But once again Luca's face flashed in front of her—the frightened, vulnerable face that had gone blank as he fell forward on the rough concrete.

She jumped up from the couch. The telephone was her only hope, her only contact with the outside. Taking the knife with her, she went back to the desk. All right, the danger was that the light would go on. She had seen her telephone repaired in the office at the Accademia. The repairman had removed the plastic cube that was the push button. She inserted the edge of the knife beneath

133

the cover, flipping it up but also breaking off the tip of the knife blade. There. There was the tiny light that she could pull out—and . . .

Idiot. That would mean that only the light on *this* telephone would not go on. It wouldn't affect the light on his phone.

She felt limp with exasperation. She knew she had only one choice. She *had* to convince McCauley that she would stay with him. A shiver of revulsion ran through her. Could she do it? Could she convince him enough that he would allow her to drive back to Florence?

Then she heard the whirr of the elevator. Looking down at the plastic cube in her hand she realized there was no time to replace it. She quickly dropped it into the pocket of her coat, left the knife on the desk, and hurried back to the couch to compose herself.

The door of the elevator opened and McCauley stepped out. The door closed behind him as he came toward her.

"That was longer than fifteen minutes," she said, going to meet him.

"Were you lonely?"

"And cold," she said, embracing him, tilting her face upward, offering her mouth.

He kissed her lightly and took both her hands in his.

"I've decided that thirty years isn't such a long time." Andrea was amazed at how normal her voice sounded.

"But fifteen minutes can be quite long," McCauley said, stepping away from her, leaving her in the middle of the room. "A great deal can happen in fifteen minutes."

"What do you mean?"

McCauley went to the panel of switches by the fireplace. Suddenly a rectangle of bars of colors appeared on the wall above the desk, accompanied by a hum that was familiar but that she could not immediately identify. The bars disappeared and in their place was a picture of a room—the room she was in.

Nothing moved for a moment, then she saw a blur that diminished and became recognizable. It was the coat on her own back. She stood frozen, watching herself on videotape.

"You can understand," McCauley said calmly, "I have to have a lot of security here."

Andrea watched the unfamiliar person on the wall go to the door and try the handle. She watched her success with the first door and her frustration with the second. Dear God, she thought, he must have a monitor in his bedroom. He's been watching me all the time he was gone.

"A little short on dialogue," McCauley said dispassionately. "No need to watch it all." He began running the tape on fast-forward. The colors jumped and blurred and blended, then separated into her likeness again. She watched with frozen fascination. The picture seemed the most obscene kind of pornography.

On the tape she left the elevator and went back to the desk, standing there, searching the room frantically with her eyes. At a moment when she bit into her lip and her face registered pure panic, McCauley froze the frame. Her terrified likeness adhered to the plaster wall like a fresco.

She turned away and dropped onto the couch.

McCauley walked leisurely to the desk and picked up the Etruscan knife. "You broke the tip of the blade, I see," he said, holding it up. "Was that on the door or the elevator or the telephone? God knows what you were trying to do to the telephone." Then he looked down and saw the exposed light bulb she had not had time to cover with the plastic cube. He laughed.

Andrea could think of nothing to say that would contradict the harsh honesty of the camera.

"So what do we do now?" McCauley crossed the room again. He stopped and stood by the fireplace, flipping the knife in the air and gracefully catching it by its jeweled handle. The sharp thin blade glinted in the fire's reflection.

"I have to assume that as soon as you left here you'd do something predictable like go to the police," he said, watching the knife flip in the air, catching it with the certainty of a juggler. "The police would not be an impossible problem, even if they insisted on searching the villa—which they would not. Your Captain Balzani may be above reproach, but the chief is a personal friend of mine." The knife flashed and arched and landed with a soft plop in his hand. "However, let's assume that the police did decide to search. There are places here in the villa and on the grounds where the painting could be hidden and never found. There would be plenty of time, because no one can enter the front gate without passing in front of the camera. The painting could be spirited away before a search party arrived at the doorstep." He flipped and caught the knife. "And think how embarrassing it would be for you—your story about the painting is losing credibility all the time.

"No," he said, fixing her in his flinty gaze, "I regret that you didn't accept my offer, because now you have become a serious problem. What am I going to do about you?"

Why didn't he put that knife down? Was he actually going to use it on her? No, of course not. Stabbing was too obvious. Stabbing was an act of passion, the solution of a vineyard worker. Clint McCauley would do nothing as untidy as stabbing.

"I could have Bud handle the problem for me," he said. "I don't believe I ever told you why Bud happens to be in Italy instead of Texas. The Houston police are still concerned about the way he solved the problem of a man who refused to pay a debt . . . some foolish barroom argument. But Bud has a strong sense of justice. He feels that when a bargain has been made it should be kept—as do I. Unfortunately, he acts from anger instead of intellect."

Flip—catch.

Yes, Andrea thought, Bud could use a knife—or a gun. He had a gun, she had seen it. He wore it strapped under his arm. He probably had used it as recently as yesterday . . . on Pietro Corsini. Had Pietro Corsini felt the explosion in his brain when the bullet hit? Had he felt his forehead crack open?

Whatever McCauley was going to do it would not be here, Andrea thought. He could force her out of the room—he could take her into the wine cellar—or the vineyard . . .

Flip—catch.

"I knew, of course, there was a possibility that I couldn't trust you," he said. "I don't often misjudge people, but I guessed wrong about you twice. You never did explain why you left Boston without calling me."

"It was because of your wife," Andrea said. She was relieved to hear the sound of her own voice.

"But you knew I had a wife."

"It was the wheelchair . . ." She did not explain further.

"For whatever reason," McCauley said evenly, "it was a disappointment to find that you were not the person I thought you were."

Flip—catch—hold. He studied the knife with its jeweled handle a moment, then placed it on the mantel above the fireplace and stood next to the portrait of David. "I think the frame is too ornate, don't you?" The cupids continued their winking and smiling in the flickering firelight. "Something of a geometric design would seem more appropriate." He looked from the picture to Andrea.

"Actually, the picture has no meaning for me now," he continued. "It's like a deer hunt. Once the beast has been tracked and shot, it becomes venison. Just as Leonardo's discarded cadavers became carrion." He took the picture from the easel and started toward her.

Could it be? Could I have misjudged him? Andrea sat stunned. He's going to give it to me! After all that, he's going to give it to me!

He stood in front of her, smiling—watching her expression. Yes, she could see that giving her the portrait would still satisfy him. It would turn her humiliation to gratitude. It would put her in his debt—regardless of how he happened to have the portrait in the first place.

She held her breath, almost afraid to move.

McCauley took one more step toward her. But instead of handing the portrait to her, in one fluid motion he opened the glass door of the fireplace and threw the framed portrait of David onto the blazing fire.

Andrea gave a strangled scream and leaped to her feet. In the split second it took for her to cross the room, he had closed the glass door and turned to catch her.

"You see," he said in the same dispassionate voice, "the problem is solved."

Andrea struggled against him, trying to kick backwards at him to free herself. Her throat throbbed and she heard her own high, thin moans.

The frame had caught on the edge of a log. Smoke quickly blackened the golden cherubs. The canvas, as yet, was intact.

"No need for the police now," McCauley was saying. "No need to call Bud."

The heat was beginning to distort the face of David. Blisters spread across his cheeks and eyes and forehead like a disfiguring disease.

The wooden frame began to flame.

Andrea struggled harder, trying with all her strength to free her arms, but McCauley pinned her securely against him. "Look on it as an episode of history interrupted," he said, his mouth next to her ear. "If the portrait had not been stolen by the priest's ancestor, this is what Savonarola would have done five hundred years ago."

Andrea stiffened in horror as the frame crackled, the flame increased and spread to the edge of the canvas. The blisters on David's contorted face boiled and burst and ran, then disappeared—like the canvas itself, fluttering up the chimney in fragments of ash.

Chapter 18

In the Pisa marina, a few boats still had lights burning in their cabins. Gino Corsini longed to be inside one of them, where a butane heater would give off warmth and cheer and where the smell of fish fried in olive oil would be as comforting as it was appetizing.

Water lapped around the sides of the sailor's church, Santa Maria della Spina, where he had spent the day hiding in an empty confessional. Now he sat in the darkened doorway, huddled against the chilling fog, listening for the sound of his uncle's skiff.

At last there was the slap of oars in the water near the ledge where he stood.

Gino got in, and neither man spoke as they skimmed across the gently moving water of the inlet and arrived at the dock on the opposite side. They tied the boat to a wooden ladder that led up to a warehouse where Pietro's car was stashed under a discarded canvas sail.

The uncle made a hurried departure, leaving Gino with a cold meatball sandwich wrapped in brown paper and an admonition to stay away from Pisa. Gino tossed the sail aside, unlocked the car, and rolled down the window before he got in and started the ignition.

The car still smelled of vomit. In the back seat were his battered suitcase, a large canvas bag, a box with his palette and paints, a collapsible easel, and two bare canvases. Gino backed through the open door of the warehouse and turned onto the blacktop road, wishing for the thousandth time that he had never let his brother Pietro get him involved in the theft of the portrait of David.

His brother's death had left Gino badly shaken. It was not that he loved Pietro so deeply. In fact, if it had ever occurred to him to analyze his feelings, he would have had to admit that he probably disliked Pietro, if not actually hated him. Pietro had always been a bully, had always ordered Gino around. Pietro had been bigger, stronger, smarter, more cunning than his younger brother.

But still there was a feeling of loss, as though Gino's own blood had drained away and seeped into the earth beneath the gravel walkway of the Leaning Tower. As degrading as he had once thought it, he had come to depend on his brother to direct his life. Pietro was the provider, Pietro the decision maker. And now that Gino was in danger, Pietro was not there to show him how to escape.

There was still physical evidence that Pietro had existed; his body lay in the morgue where their uncle had gone to identify it. But what about his mind—his thoughts? Did they stay behind, too? Was it simply that the fabric that held the mind and body together had unraveled and the essence of his brother was still here?

Gino did not believe nor disbelieve in the supernatural, but he needed no outside help to predict what his brother's response would be to any situation. *Go to Naples*, his brother would have said. *Go and stay with Aunt Renata on the dairy farm.*

But how? Gino had no money.

Get in touch with Leo Fozzi. Demand enough to get away.

On the corner of the street ahead was a red telephone booth next to a lighted Exxon sign with one of the *X*s missing. Gino pulled the car to the curb in the dense shadow of a poplar tree. There was no light inside the booth, but he dialed zero and gave the operator the number he wanted in Florence.

"Albion Hotel." It was Leo Fozzi who answered.

Gino hesitated.

Go ahead and tell him, idiot. He has more reason to be afraid of you than you have to be afraid of him.

"This is Gino. I need money. I'm going to Naples."

There was a long pause. Then Fozzi said, "Are you crazy? Why are you calling me?"

"I need money."

"I can't talk to you." Fozzi's voice was an exaggerated whisper. "I have an engagement party booked in the dining room. People are beginning to arrive . . ."

Don't let him get away with that!

"Pietro still had the payment for the portrait with him when he was shot," Gino said. "I can't very well go to the police and demand it."

"Stay with your uncle. I will drive over tomorrow and bring you what I can."

"I can't stay with . . ." Gino began, but Fozzi had already hung up. Gino stood holding the dead instrument in his hand.

He can't treat you that way. Call him again. Tell him the police are watching the boat. Insist that he bring the money tonight.

Gino placed another call.

"Albion Hotel."

"I can't stay here. The police are watching the boat. I spent the day hiding in a church."

"All right, all right. I'll meet you tomorrow morning in Pisa at the Solferino Bridge." Fozzi hung up again.

Call him again.

Gino returned to the car. Tomorrow, Fozzi had said.

He would bring the money tomorrow. That would be time enough. But Gino knew Pietro would not sit and wait for Fozzi. Fozzi might not show up at all.

Drive to Florence tonight. Make Fozzi give you cash.

Gino steered the car onto Via Cattaneo, and headed for the back road to Florence through Cascina.

Stay off the autostrada. Watch out for heavy traffic and speed traps.

The shroud of fog clung to the marina, but as Gino got farther away the sky was clear, and as he picked up speed a cold wind lashed against his face through the open window. The wind made his eyes blink and tear, but it was better than the smell of the closed car.

All Gino had ever wanted was to study at the Accademia. Pietro had made that possible by paying his tuition. Pietro had told him, "I suppose you may as well spend your time in class as anywhere else. But you will never be an artist—even your instructor says you're a follower, not an originator of style."

But to his brother's credit, Gino had to admit, Pietro had never pushed him to join his black market business—not because Pietro wanted to spare him from a life of crime, but because Gino was emotional and unpredictable when he was challenged. He would run—dissolve into tears—or, as he had done the night of the theft, vomit when he was really frightened. But Pietro had needed his brother's help for the theft of the portrait. Gino, as a student at the Accademia, knew the floor plan well, and Luca, the guard assigned to the first floor basement where the safe was, was Gino's friend.

The plan had been formulated by Leo Fozzi and Pietro—on contract, Pietro told Gino, from an American. A simple matter, they had said—there would be no problems. But who could have guessed that Vittorio Sassetti and those other people would have come down in the elevator while Gino and Pietro were still there?

CASCINA—3 KILOMETERS. The sign appeared in his headlights around the bend of the road.

You would be safe if it were not for the signorina with the red hair.

It was true. She was the only one who could identify him. She had seen his face.

Pietro would have already handled that problem if he were alive. Gino still could not believe that Pietro had let himself get killed. And who had done it? Surely not the signorina. Then who?

Not Leo Fozzi. Fozzi was almost as big a coward as Gino. Conceivably he might secretly poison someone's food, but he would never have the nerve to shoot someone in a public place in broad daylight. It must have been the American who bought the painting. Gino did not know who the American was, and he did not want to know. He shuddered at the possibility of meeting his brother's killer. The thought was more frightening than being caught by the police.

But the American does not know you. He has never seen you. Your only threat is the signorina.

Gino reached across the passenger seat and opened the glove compartment. The gun Pietro had made him take to the basement of the Accademia was inside.

The road curved along with the Arno as he approached Empoli. There was no question about what Pietro would do about the signorina.

Wait—be calm—find an opportunity.

Soon Gino was at the outskirts of Florence. As he entered the city he kept to the back streets until he turned into the down ramp of the Albion Hotel's subterranean garage.

Pietro would have advised him that it was foolhardy to go inside and look for Leo Fozzi now. There was a party going on in the dining room. Music punctuated with jagged laughter pounded and pierced the brick walls. Far better to wait here until Fozzi came out.

He parked behind the hotel's VW sightseeing bus where he could not be seen from the hotel doorway or the entrance to the garage. Yes, he would wait. If there were no chance to see Fozzi before 7:15, Gino knew that every morning at that time the hotel proprietor came through the garage to check on the storeroom and order supplies.

Suddenly Gino felt hungry. Remembering the meatball sandwich, he peeled away the paper and began to eat—quickly but with little enjoyment. He had just finished when he saw a flash of light reflected on the ceiling as a car entered the garage and headed down the ramp.

Gino ducked out of sight as a late arrival in a red Alfa Romeo drove by and parked in a reserved slot near the back entrance. Cautiously Gino raised himself up enough to peer out the window. He watched the back of the woman driver's quilted brocade coat as she walked swiftly toward the door. As she entered, Gino recognized her. He had thought he knew her earlier just by the color of her hair.

Open the glove compartment . . .

Gino opened the glove compartment again and removed the gun, stuffing it into the waistband of his trousers.

The door to the Albion's dining room was open. Andrea glanced in as she crossed the lobby to the stairs. Her mind was a camera's open shutter; images crowded in one on top of the other, leaving no room for memory. She saw a swirl of moving bodies—colorful dresses, black tuxedos, dancing to a popular ballad from an American movie. In the instant it took to pass the doorway, Andrea saw the glint of the trumpet as the soloist stood at the microphone, his youthful brow covered with sweat. She saw the sign above

145

his head, *"Congratulations Mario and Lucia."* A waiter with a towel-wrapped bottle weaved in and out of the throng filling proffered glasses. A girl in a pink chiffon dress slipped on the dance floor and was pulled upright by her embarrassed escort. A smiling gray-haired lady was wearing a floral print dress that conformed to the rolls of fat around her abdomen and buttocks and showed too much wrinkled, protruding bosom. The handsome young man whose arm the woman held looked as though he desperately wanted to escape.

Approaching the stairs, Andrea turned toward the back door. The chandelier of the lobby was reflected in the top half of the glass. Lower on the glass was the cream-colored vinyl couch. Between the two images, she saw a face. A face that was not a reflection—a face, indistinct in the shadows but somehow familiar—a face looking in from outside.

Andrea did not try to remember where she had seen the man before. Her memory was not a companion whose company she wanted. Paying inordinate attention to externals was the only way she had been able to perform the routine function of driving away from McCauley's villa. She had counted the number of curves in the road. She had identified the trees that moved toward, then behind her in the headlights. When she reached the city, she noted how many delivery trucks were on the streets, how many yellow cars, how many motorcycles before she got to the garage of the Albion.

She continued up the stairs to her room. The face she had seen in the door passed through her mind along with the many other images from the party in the dining room. She was grateful that she got to her room without meeting anyone.

When the last fragment of the portrait of David had been burned and only chunks of the wooden frame were left in the fireplace, McCauley had released his hold on her. She had stood numb, still staring into the fire. Seconds later she heard the whirr of the elevator and turned to see the door closing with McCauley inside.

She listened as it traveled to the upper floor. The door slid open. Then there was a slice of silence. Then one of the few emotions Andrea hadn't felt that evening bubbled up. She was angry! She went to the middle of the room and faced where the camera would be. "Open that damn door and let me out of here!" she demanded.

The outside doors automatically opened, and when she reached the landing she saw that her car was parked at the foot of the stairs by the wine cellar.

Now, as she opened the door to her room at the Albion she concentrated on a familiar squeak that usually annoyed her. Somehow it seemed strangely reassuring.

She knew nothing could restore the portrait of David. And even though McCauley was an *Ubermensch* whose wealth allowed him to live above the law, she had to take some action.

Before she stepped into the shower to wash what she could of the evening away, she reached for the telephone, read the number pasted on the cradle and dialed.

Chapter 19

Captain Aldo Balzani waited until after the two kidnappers had been booked, then went to his office to close out the file on the missing wealthy cinema producer. He had been found dead, locked in the trunk of a car parked in the public lot of the Stazione Centrale. At least Balzani's men had been able to capture the killers from careless evidence (fingerprints and a packet of matches) left with the body.

Balzani picked up a ballpoint pen and began to write in the file folder. The pen stopped working. Balzani sighed and threw it in the wastebasket. Sometimes it seemed that nothing in the whole city—the country, for that matter—worked properly.

Five years was not long enough to erase his appreciation of American efficiency. And though in New Orleans, where he grew up, the pace of the city was set by the sluggish Mississippi River, at least the telephones worked, the stores opened and closed at regular hours, and if the tap said "hot," the water was.

Balzani looked around his office. The window was stuck open two inches. The letters v and l and the number 6 on his typewriter stuck and had to be pulled away from the platen by hand. The cord on his gooseneck lamp had shorted out, and the bottom drawer of his desk would not open.

He knew it was useless to complain to the maintenance man. He would get the same response he got when he complained to his landlord about the laundry service that was always late . . . or the postman who delivered his mail to the wrong address (if at all) . . . or to the manager of the cheese market when the provoloni was moldy. Always, it was a shrug of the shoulders—hands held up in resignation, as if to say, "Why should you ask so much of life?"

"I'm checking out now, Captain," one of the arresting officers said from the open doorway.

"Fine." Balzani watched as the officer put on his slightly pointed brown helmet and retreated down the hall. The pointed hats and the brown uniforms of the Florentine policemen made them look like oversized gnomes, in Balzani's opinion.

That was one good thing. At least he didn't have to wear a uniform. He had four durable—though outdated—three-piece suits that he wore alternately. All his shirts were white, all his socks were black and his ties were of muted colors that would blend with anything, so that assembling his wardrobe was never a problem. Indeed, he could—and often did—dress in the dark.

His clothes had bored Lili Matucci, who spent most of her check from the chorus of the small opera company at the fashion boutiques along Via dei Calzaiuoli. When they were out together her eyes always followed a man in a Fila tennis jacket or a Cesarani suit. Maybe the assistant conductor's white dinner jacket was the reason she had married him.

The thought of Lili no longer brought the rush of pain to Balzani that it once had, but still, it was something he preferred not to deal with. He found a pencil with a broken point in the center drawer of his desk, sharpened it with his pocket knife, and had started on the file folder again when the phone rang.

"Balzani," he answered, sounding almost as tired as he felt.

"This is Andrea Perkins."

"Oh? I'll be damned. How can I help you, ma'am?"

"Probably you can't. But I'd like to talk with you just the same."

"Of course. When?"

"Tonight."

"Tonight?" The captain slung the pencil and the file folder in the middle drawer and closed it. "Well, now . . . I was just getting around to having dinner. How would it be if you met me at . . . do you know Ristorante Nandina?"

"Yes."

"Thirty minutes?"

"Fine."

The music had stopped in the dining room of the Albion Hotel. Gino Corsini could hear a slurred voice over the microphone proposing a toast to the engaged couple and the hubbub of the crowd that refused to be quiet and listen.

Gino sat in the corner of the passenger's side of his car—in the shadow of the overhead fluorescent light in the garage. Taking the gun from the waistband of his trousers he put it on the seat. Then he moved his long fingers across it, becoming familiar with the shape—the curve of the trigger—the weight of the handle.

After a time he glanced back at the door into the Albion and saw it open a crack. His hand tightened around the gun, then relaxed when he saw a young couple from the engagement party. The boy embraced the girl, kissing her neck, his hands on her back, then creeping up and slipping one of the straps of her evening dress off her shoulder.

"Lasciami stare," the girl giggled in a voice that did not sound as though she wanted him to leave her alone.

They straightened and stood apart as the door opened again and the signorina with the red hair came out.

Gino tightened his grip on the handle. Of course he could not use the gun in the presence of the young couple. But this was a test of sorts—to see if he had the courage to use it at all.

He caught a glimpse of his own eyes in the rearview mirror. He was startled to see that they could have been those of his brother, Pietro. The warmth of Gino's eyes, which he had once accurately recorded in a self-portrait, was gone. In its place was a furtiveness, a determination.

The signorina backed her car and turned up the exit ramp. She had changed her clothes—which meant that she lived here, Gino thought quickly. Should he follow her?

No. Don't take a chance on being seen by the police! Wait. She lives here. You can be ready for her when she comes back.

Chapter 20

Ristorante Nandina was at 1 Piazza Santa Trinità, a narrow, medieval street. Even at this late hour the public parking lot where Andrea left her Alfa Romeo was crowded with the cars of restaurant customers who stayed to hear the trio that played there four nights a week.

As she hurried to cross the darkened street she stumbled sightly, misjudging the height of the curb. A firm hand caught her elbow and Aldo Balzani said, "You're right on time."

Andrea couldn't see his face clearly, but she recognized the drawl. "Yes," she said, relieved that it was he.

At the corner, a sign in red neon script read, *Ristorante Nandina* and hung above an unpretentious entrance to the cellar café. Balzani opened the door, and they stood in a small foyer at the top of a stairway.

Balzani preceded Andrea down narrow stone steps to a basement room that seemed to vibrate with the music of the trio and the conversation and laughter of the customers. Sconces with amber chimneys were affixed halfway up the walls at irregular intervals, and their candles cast a soft glow. The ceiling was hidden by a profusion of hanging copper pots, strings of onions, and empty raffia-covered Chianti bottles. A stucco arch curved above the open kitchen and was outlined with a vertical brick design.

The aroma of garlic, spicy sausage, and pungent sauces drifted in from the steamy kitchen.

On a low platform opposite the entrance were three musicians, playing "Come Back to Sorrento" on accordion, mandolin, and guitar.

"That song is for the tourists," Balzani told Andrea. "After hours they play Dixieland jazz that would convince you you're on Bourbon Street."

"Aldo!" A plump, short, middle-aged woman in a red apron came running out of the kitchen, her arms open. Her black hair was pulled so tightly into a knot at the back of her head it seemed to stretch and flatten her features and gave her face the rounded contour of a melon.

"Nandina!" Balzani reached down to hug her, then lifted her briefly and planted a noisy kiss on her cheek. When he set her down, she grinned girlishly and smoothed her already sleek hair.

"Ah, Aldo," she said with a deep sigh and the expression of a mourner, "it is too long since you were here."

"Nandina . . . this is Signorina Andrea Perkins." Then turning to Andrea, Balzani said, "This is my cousin Nandina, who, as a child in the city of Potenza was touched by a witch's wand and given the power to make the best ricotta ravioli in all Italy."

Nandina beamed at him, then took Andrea by the hand. "Come with me." She pushed through a group of young men standing near the doorway and shouted over her shoulder at Balzani, "I saved the booth in the corner for you."

It wasn't easy getting through the crowded basement room, but at last they were seated in a curved maroon vinyl booth. The guitarist on the nearby platform yelled a greeting to Balzani, who smiled and waved back at him.

From a service counter Nandina produced wineglasses, silverware, ironstone plates, and then with a flourish, draped crisp white napkins across the laps of Andrea and Balzani. "First I bring you wine and pasta," she said, pinching Balzani's cheek, "then you sing for us."

The police captain protested, but his cousin turned her back and retreated to the kitchen.

"A singing policeman?" Andrea said.

"Only when I'm off duty." Balzani broke a breadstick and offered half to her. "Crooks don't take you seriously if you sing."

Andrea laughed in spite of herself, refusing the breadstick.

"You're not hungry?"

"No." Her stomach was still churning from the ordeal at McCauley's villa.

Balzani leaned his head back and stretched his legs beneath the table. He gave in to the tiredness of an eighteen-hour day and prepared to take on another problem in as comfortable a fashion as possible. "Well then, what was so urgent that you wanted to talk to me tonight?"

Andrea hesitated for a moment, then plunged into an expurgated account of her evening. The story she had left was a skeleton whose bones were: McCauley had offered her a job as curator of his museum. She had accepted. He had shown her the portrait of David and expected her to keep his secret. She had refused. He had burned the painting. She added that the painting had been obtained in Pisa by McCauley's nephew, Bud, and that she suspected that Bud was the one who had shot Pietro Corsini.

Nandina suddenly reappeared with a tray that held a carafe of red wine and a platter with mounds of plump, neatly crimped ravioli and stacks of glistening sausages. She placed the platter squarely between Balzani and Andrea, then smiled proudly as she poured the wine, whispering to Balzani loud enough for Andrea to hear, "*Bella* signorina." Then once again, she was gone, hurrying to greet a noisy group that had just entered the foyer.

Balzani picked up a heavy serving fork and put a small portion of ravioli and sausage onto Andrea's plate—over her protestations. "That's to please Nandina," he said, generously serving himself. "She'd never believe anyone—no matter what the circumstances—would refuse to eat her ravioli." He took a large swallow of wine and pointed to Andrea's glass. "Try it," he said.

Andrea sipped the flinty liquid. It was rough and tart but warming and richly grapey.

"Nandina's brother has a small winery down near Siena," Balzani said, beginning to attack the pile of pasta in front of him. "It's nothing like the high-tech wineries of California, but he makes a pretty darn good wine, don'cha think?"

Why, Andrea thought incredulously, is he talking to me about wineries? She had just described a horror-filled evening at McCauley's villa, and Balzani seemed not even to have heard her.

"This isn't for sipping." Balzani poured more wine for himself and frowned at Andrea's almost full glass. "Drink it."

"You don't believe me, do you?" She was suddenly bordering on hysteria. "You don't believe a thing I told you."

The police captain turned and looked directly into her eyes and said in dead seriousness, "I think you were damn lucky to get out of there alive."

He picked up Andrea's glass and handed it to her, waited until she drained it then filled it again.

"It's not, after all, the question of the cat and the Giotto." His voice was casual again, giving her a chance to collect her composure. "Have you heard that old favorite of the Florentine philosophy professors? If you were trapped in a burning building with a painting by Giotto and a mangy cat, and you could only save one . . . which one would you save?"

The trio concluded an up-tempo version of "Ciao Venezia" and moved smoothly into the sentimental "O Sole Mio."

"Of course no one can predict how he will react in a crisis," Balzani said as he filled his plate from the platter again. "Considering that you are a professional in the art world, I don't know what your answer would be. But I'm pretty sure what I'd do. I'd grab the cat—clawing and screeching—and head for the fire escape." He refilled Andrea's glass. "Drink it," he said.

"It's not that I'm crazy about cats," he continued. "Once we hit the alley, I'd let him go and he could fend for himself. It's just that I think life is more important than art." The police captain paused, serving himself a sausage, "But a man who would deliberately destroy a work of art is either sick, like the fellow who took a hammer to the *Pietà* in the Vatican some years ago, or he has no regard for humanity. In either case, he's dangerous. Now, let's start with when you were first given the painting. Tell me everything you can remember."

Prodded by Balzani's questions, Andrea recounted the entire series of events. The longer she spoke, the more absurd her story sounded—even to her. The theft and her kidnapping—her escape from the Corsini brother—the phony portrait they had examined the morning before at the Accademia—the fact that the portrait of David had finally turned up in the unlikely setting of McCauley's villa—and that he had burned it. Who could believe any of it?

When she had finished, Balzani sat retracing a figure eight with the base of his wineglass on the tablecloth. He said nothing.

Were his eyes deliberately avoiding her? "You don't

really believe me, do you?" she asked.

"It doesn't matter whether I do or not." He turned toward her with the fragment of a smile. "As it happens . . . I do."

"Thank you." She knew her response was odd, but she could think of no other way to express the gratitude she felt that someone considered her both honest and sane. "What can we do about it?" she asked finally.

"Nothing."

"Nothing?"

"There's no evidence. Pietro Corsini is dead—so he can't tell us who hired him to steal the portrait. His brother, Gino, has disappeared. If he is apprehended, we'll at least have a starting place, but who can say when—or if—he'll *he* apprehended. As for Pietro's death . . . no one actually saw who shot him. No one can even say that Bud McCauley was on the sidewalk at the time, so I can hardly charge him with murder."

"What about searching McCauley's villa?" Andrea asked.

"On what grounds?"

"Couldn't you check Bud's gun to see if it matches the bullet that killed Pietro? He always carries a gun—he's McCauley's bodyguard."

"By the time we got through the gate and up to the villa, any gun could be disposed of—unless McCauley's nephew had no reason to fear its being examined."

Andrea knew his arguments were valid, but she couldn't give up. "What about analyzing the ashes in McCauley's fireplace. The age of a canvas can be established from ash . . ."

"What good would that do? Even if we proved that the canvas was five hundred years old, it could have been a finger-painting done by a child in a Renaissance nursery school. There's no way to establish from the ashes that it was painted by Michelangelo, is there?"

"No." Andrea sighed and put down her wineglass, which was immediately refilled—this time by Nandina. She stood over Andrea, frowning at the plate that still held the single raviolo and sausage that Balzani had put there.

"That was her third helping," Balzani said. "She tried, but couldn't finish it."

"Yes," Andrea smiled weakly at the now beaming cook, "It was marvelous."

"Just simple country food," Nandina replied with false modesty. "Now Aldo," she said, taking Balzani's arm and tugging him upright, "for *me* you must sing."

He grinned at Andrea. "It's better than paying the tab."

Nandina pulled him by the hand to the bandstand.

The trio of musicians greeted him warmly. After conferring briefly, the mandolin player began an intricate introduction. His fingers flexed and flattened against the strings. To Andrea, the music had the same stridency as the wine.

The crowd quieted in expectation. Balzani was completely at ease and obviously enjoying himself. He stretched out one arm and put his right hand over his heart. His chest visibly filled with air and his mouth opened like a cavern. One note and one word came out.

"When . . ." he sang, his voice booming through the small room, rumbling and vibrating against the tinkling single chord that the mandolin repeated until Balzani's lungs were empty. He held the pitch a full thirty seconds, giving the crowd time to speculate. Would he sing a traditional Italian song? An operatic aria?

He sang, one tone lower, "the . . ." Then more obbligato from the mandolin player, who on Balzani's cue settled into a vigorous waltz tempo as the police captain sang,

". . . moon hits your eye like a big pizza pie, that's amore . . ."

The audience laughed and applauded. It was a curious mixture of Pavarotti and Dean Martin—and, Andrea thought, altogether wonderful. When Balzani finished, the crowd would not let him leave until they sang a second chorus with him.

Andrea and Balzani spoke no more about McCauley that evening. Nandina saw to it that the carafe of wine was not allowed to get empty as they talked quietly of New Orleans and Boston—but with no homesickness. The later the hour got, the more content they both were to be exactly where they were.

"Are you all right?" Balzani asked when he saw her to her car.

"Yes."

"Not too much wine?"

"No, really." But his face did look a little fuzzy to her.

Then he leaned into the car window and in a serious tone said, "I'll follow you to your hotel and watch until you get inside. Be sure to lock the door to your room."

"I will." Andrea rolled up the window and turned to leave. Yes, she thought, he would choose to save the cat . . . and she wondered if she would have the strength of character to make the same choice.

Chapter 21

Because of the wine, Andrea had to stoop down, her eyes level with the lock, in order to see how to fit the key in the door to her room. On the second try the door swung open with its familiar squeak.

She had never been particularly concerned for her own safety, but the events of the past few days made her determined to have a dead bolt installed as soon as possible. That decided, she dismissed the possibility of danger and thought of the evening she had spent with Aldo Balzani.

As she undressed, she smiled to herself. He certainly was not the government-issue Italian policeman she had thought him to be. He had made her laugh, and she still felt a euphoria that was not entirely due to the wine. But the feeling of well-being that he engendered did not have a chance of surviving in this room that was crowded with reminders of McCauley. The protective wall she had built around her thoughts fell away like stones without mortar when she glanced at a stack of books on her desk—the top one, a Rizzoli catalogue of the works of Michelangelo.

She dropped onto the bed, unable to combat the memory of the burning portrait. The image of the fire stayed and grew, like the obscene blisters that had covered David's face, bubbles that spread and broke like pustules, releasing a yellow liquid before the flame consumed the canvas.

But something in the scene was inconsistent. What? She had the same sort of feeling she might get if she noticed someone in a Renaissance painting wearing a wristwatch. In shutting out the grotesqueness of her evening with McCauley, Andrea had also shut out logic. And then she realized what she had been too shocked to see before. *The blisters should not have been there!* It would have been impossible in a five-hundred-year-old painting. There would have been no moisture left!

She threw her head back and heard the sound of her own laughter. What she had seen was melting resin! That's what it had to have been. Just as in the portrait she had examined at the Accademia the morning before, the pigment was suspended in formaldehyde resin. McCauley's painting was a fake, too!

She could not stop laughing. At least she thought she was laughing. That's what it felt like . . . but her cheeks were wet.

What she did next she later blamed on the wine. But even if she had not still felt a little giddy, her first impulse would have been to confront McCauley with what she had discovered. Though in a more sober moment she might not have acted on it.

She took the card from her billfold and dialed his direct number, then listened as each digit was locked in electronically, followed by a buzz at the other end. The phone was picked up almost instantly.

"Yes?" McCauley said with no trace of sleep in his voice.

"It's Andrea Perkins."

"This is a surprise."

She was aware that her voice sounded strange—breathy with excitement and lower than usual. "I won't keep you long. I just want you to know that the painting you burned was a fake." She paused for a reply, but there was none. "If you have any doubts that what I've told you is true, have the ashes analyzed in the Mc36." Then she calmly hung up.

She had never felt so elated. She was sure McCauley believed he had destroyed an original painting by Michelangelo. Playing tricks was not his style. Power plays were what he enjoyed. This was probably as close to justice as McCauley would ever come. Andrea thought—but at least she had the satisfaction that he had been fooled, and, belatedly, that she had not.

The tiredness she had ignored for days suddenly seemed irresistible. She changed into her nightgown and stretched out on the bed. For a second before she slipped into a deep and even sleep, she remembered the music of a tinkling mandolin accompanying a confident, booming baritone.

Chapter 22

McCauley held the dead receiver for several seconds before replacing it. Was what she told him true? Her voice had had a quality he had never heard in it before. The sibilants were breathy, the *t*s indistinct. Had she drunk too much and decided on some obscure form of revenge? He did not think so.

He *could* have the ashes analyzed. No, she was sure of what she told him, or she would not have called. But how could she know that the painting was a fake? She had been convinced that it was genuine when she watched it burn.

McCauley paced the room. Why, now, was she sure that it wasn't genuine? He sat on the side of his bed frowning, and then grinned at what he decided was the answer. The only way she could be sure it was a fake, he thought, was if she had learned where the original was. Someone had sold Bud a phony. Yes, she knew where the original was—but she did not have it yet! Wouldn't she have told him if she did? Wouldn't she have said that the painting had been returned to the Accademia and that she would prove its authenticity with the Mc36?

"So," he said out loud, "it's still hunting season."

She was the trophy he had wanted. But she had eluded him. She had also escaped the revenge that was almost as sweet as capture.

He picked up the phone again and dialed, getting an answer after the second ring.

"Yeah?" his nephew growled, and coughed into the phone.

"Bud, you were cheated."

"Huh?"

"Whoever sold you that painting gave you a ringer."

"Are you sure?"

Clint McCauley did not reply.

"How do you know?"

After a brief but significant pause, the uncle said, "For your own well-being, you had better deal with the thief who sold it to you."

"Yes, sir."

"And Bud, even more important, keep track of that woman Andrea Perkins. She knows where the real one is."

"I will, sir."

"Bring the car around tomorrow morning at seven. Daley and I are going back to Houston."

Gino Corsini dozed fitfully in the garage of the Albion Hotel. The temperature had dropped as he slept, and the cold had wakened him. He pressed his palms together and clamped his hands between his knees. He was always conscious of protecting his hands—from the cold, from burns, from cuts or scratches. His hands were his existence. He was a painter—no matter what his brother Pietro said.

The city was quiet. The only sounds from the street were those of trucks making early-morning deliveries.

Gino thought of the classroom at the Accademia. He thought of the tripod easel he rolled from window to window searching for the perfect light. His instructor said Gino had an excellent eye for color and attention to detail. Gino was proud of his almost infallible sense of proportion of pigment to mix to achieve the shade he wanted.

The VW bus next to his car, for instance; it was not just *blue*. To mix its color he would start with as much flake white as the tip of his palette knife would hold, then mix in a third as much Prussian blue and an eighth as much burnt sienna. And he would get it right the first time—not like the students the instructor was always praising for their *fresh concepts* and *individuality*.

Thinking of the combination of colors used in the blue of the bus reminded him that his last tube of flake white was almost empty. He thought of stopping by the art supply store after class tomorrow. Then he was shunted back to reality. As long as he could be identified by the signorina, he would never be able to go back to class. It was then that he noticed her car was in the garage again.

He felt for the gun he had left beside him in the seat.

He held the weapon in front of him in the palm of his hand. Its silvery shine drew the colors around it into it. The blue from the bus was reflected across the top of the barrel. The pink and white shades of his own hand lit and warmed the underside. The weapon looked less like an instrument of evil than a mirror of the world around it.

Suddenly, headlights appeared at the down ramp of the garage. Gino slouched in the seat, catching a glimpse of a black Ferrari that pulled in and parked in a spot reserved for delivery trucks. A man in denim pants and leather jacket got out and went quickly inside. Who could he be, Gino wondered idly. If he lived at the hotel, he would have his own reserved parking space. Obviously he was not delivering anything in a Ferrari.

A few minutes later the man returned. Someone was with him. When they crossed under the light above the door, Gino could see that the second man was Leo Fozzi—stuffing his shirt into his pants, his sparse hair falling into his eyes.

The man in the leather jacket opened the door of the Ferrari. Gino could not hear the conversation, but could tell that Fozzi was protesting. The other man gave Fozzi's shoulder a push, and at last the hotel owner got into the car.

Then the man in the leather jacket hurried to the driver's side and started the engine. The car sped out of the garage with its unwilling passenger.

Gino sat back, dropping the gun onto the seat beside him, then massaging his hands. What had he just seen? Who was the man in the leather jacket who could force Fozzi to go with him? A relative? Someone in the family could be sick. A black market customer demanding merchandise? But in the pit of his stomach, Gino knew that neither of those speculations was right.

Oh, God, what would Pietro do?

Pietro would find a way out. He always had. No—not always. He had not escaped from the man in Pisa. The man in the black Ferrari?

A wave of nausea swept over Gino.

But what would Pietro do?

Gino admitted to himself that the man with Fozzi must have been the American.

Where were they going? Why had he come for Fozzi in the middle of the night?

Gino's stomach made a convulsive jump when he thought . . . he'll come after me next.

The American does not know who you are!

That's right. He has never seen me.

The only thing you have to worry about is the girl.

Yes. And she is somewhere in the hotel right now.

Find the girl. Once she's out of the way—you're free.

Gino gripped the gun, then stuffed it into his waistband and buttoned his jacket over it. Cautiously he got out of the car and looked around the garage to make sure he was alone before starting for the hotel entrance.

How could he find her? He did not know her name. Yes. Yes, he did. He had seen it on a list of employees at the Accademia—but he could not remember what it was. It sounded like a color—a gemstone . . . but he could not remember.

Look at the names on the mailboxes behind the reception desk. You might recognize it.

Gino eased the door to the hotel open. The lobby was empty and dark except for the light above the revolving door and the green-shaded lamp on the reception desk. Through the glass of the front door he could see the fading sky—like a canvas of flat gray gesso.

Hurry! People will be milling about soon.

He crept behind the desk, running his finger beneath the mailboxes, reading the names. Finally, he found it. Ambrea . . . Amber . . . Andrea. Yes, that was it. Andrea Perkins.

See if there is a key in the box.

He reached inside and felt the metal key attached to a plastic disk. Albion Hotel, 207.

Stay on the carpeted part of the stairs.

Gino quietly climbed the single flight, clutching the wooden railing. He stopped at the first door and looked at the number—200. He could hear someone snoring inside.

The other side of the hall—look on the other side.

Halfway down he spotted number 207. He put his ear to the door and listened. He could hear a clock ticking, but that was all. Maybe she wasn't there, he thought almost hopefully. Putting the plastic disk of the key between his teeth, he rubbed his hands down his trouser legs to wipe the sweat off his palms. Then, with infinite care, he put the key into the lock.

Slowly. Turn it slowly. And twist the knob as soon as you hear it click.

He did, and the door opened a fraction. A hinge squeaked as he pushed the door wider and crept inside. The room was dark, but the unbroken gray of the sky that was growing lighter seeped through a torn window shade. He flattened himself against the wall for a moment, holding his breath, getting his bearings, adjusting to the half-light.

Across the room the signorina lay on the bed, her face to the wall. Her red hair was spread across the empty pillow next to her—flake white . . . equal parts of raw sienna and carmine.

There is not much time!

Dropping the key into his pocket, Gino took the gun from his waistband. How can I shoot her and escape? The sound will bring people from all over the hotel.

Put the gun to her neck and cover her head with a pillow before you fire—that will deaden the sound.

What if she struggles?

There won't be time.

Gino eased toward the bed. He calculated that he would need four steps. One . . . two . . . three . . . The signorina moaned softly and turned in her sleep, facing him, flinging her arm across the edge of the bed, her hand grazing his leg. Gino froze—not breathing or moving, hearing her breathe.

He could touch her. Ivory skin with a hint of cadmium yellow and scarlet.

Pick up the pillow.

Gino looked at his hands as though he expected them to work independently of him. His head felt light. He was dizzy.

Pick up the pillow! Use the gun, then drop it on the bed and leave!

Reaching across Andrea's body, Gino gently lifted the pillow from the bed. He positioned it over the hand that held the gun so that the larger portion would cover her head.

Her blood would be pure scarlet . . . scarlet that spread on the sheet and darkened her hair to burnt umber. And then . . . And then Gino defied Pietro.

His own instincts were too strong.

He could imagine Pietro's advice, but he could not imitate his actions. As always in a crisis, he ran.

Pietro's accusing voice rang in his ears, *Idiot! Go back! It is your only chance.*

Gino fled down the hall, down the stairs, into the garage.

She is the one who can stop you from painting!

A bread truck had just pulled into the spot reserved for deliveries. *"Buon giorno,"* a man in a white uniform said, balancing a box on his shoulder as he stepped out of the truck's rear door.

Gino ran past him, holding his hand over his mouth.

"That must have been some party," the man grinned and pushed the service door to the hotel with his other shoulder.

Chapter 23

It was well after eight in the morning when Andrea woke, and would have slept even longer except for the ringing of the telephone. The caller was Captain Aldo Balzani.

They chatted briefly about the evening before, agreeing that they might have had too much wine but neither of them regretting a drop of it.

"I have a request to make of you," Balzani said in a more businesslike tone.

And I have something to tell you, Andrea thought, remembering her call to McCauley.

"We arrested Gino Corsini this morning. I'd like you to come down and identify him."

Balzani told her that Gino had been arrested by a policeman on routine patrol who recognized him from a student ID picture circulated throughout the department. "He was standing outside the Accademia talking with some of his classmates," Balzani told her, adding, "He must have thought it was too obvious a place for us to look for him."

Andrea dressed quickly, but carefully, and left. Yesterday she would have made this trip to the police station with a sense of dread. Now, she hurried down the hallway humming happily to herself as she went to identify a man who was a thief and a kidnapper.

*　　　*　　　*

"Wine treats you kindly," Captain Balzani said as Andrea entered his office. "You look wonderful."

Momentarily, Andrea reverted to a stammer she had conquered in puberty. "I . . . I slept well," she said, accepting the usual battered chair. "The wine helped . . . and a discovery I made."

Balzani sat on the corner of his desk as she told him how she had realized the painting McCauley burned was a fake. The detective grinned at her story until she mentioned the call to McCauley. "You called and told him?" he asked, his brows suddenly at attention.

"If my head had been clearer I probably wouldn't have," Andrea said. "But I felt a need for immediate revenge."

Rubbing the side of his nose thoughtfully, Balzani asked, "Do you think he knew all along that it was a fake?"

"I thought of that, but, no." She watched her fingers as they lightly tapped the edge of the desk. "I think he believed it was actually painted by Michelangelo. He got some perverse sense of power from destroying it."

"I'm sorry you called him," Balzani said. Why had she? Didn't she realize how dangerous a man like McCauley could be? On the other hand, could any woman think of someone whose bed she had shared—someone she loved—thought she loved—as dangerous?

Balzani had deduced that there had been more than a business relationship between Andrea and McCauley. He had guessed from the way her eyes would never meet his when she mentioned McCauley's name, and from the way her fingers found something distracting to do when she spoke of him—like twist a strand of hair, smooth an eyebrow, tap lightly on the desk . . . as she was doing now.

Hadn't Balzani felt the same need to repay pain with pain, humiliation with humiliation, when Lili married her assistant conductor? The most satisfying thing that happened after Lili had left was reading the scathing review of her husband's performance when he filled in for the ailing conductor. "His authority and presence on the podium inspired the audience to double its prayers for the health of the maestro." Ah, yes . . . it still gave Balzani pleasure to remember it.

But a man like McCauley could be dangerous. He would not take failure lightly.

So that he would not transfer his uneasiness to Andrea, Balzani changed the subject to the reason he had asked her to the police station. "Do you feel uncomfortable about identifying Gino Corsini?"

She admitted that she did. It wasn't fear—certainly not here in the police station. She doubted that she would have been frightened of Gino even if they had met unexpectedly in some deserted place. There was something pathetic about him—something soft and suffering that she did not want to see again.

Balzani preceded her down the hall. They stopped in front of a door marked *Interrogazione*. Before he opened it Balzani said, "Once you've identified Corsini, you're free to leave."

"If it's all right, I'd rather stay." Quickly she added, "He must know where the original painting is."

"Possibly."

"Whatever the case, I'd like to stay."

Balzani shrugged, and opened the door.

The room was as grim as its reason for being. It was windowless and had only one door. There were four bare walls of flaking gray paint. The light that was suspended from the ceiling was fluorescent and negated shadow, allowing no illusions. There was nothing in the room to distract, no place to hang imagination.

The room did not invite small talk, and neither Andrea

nor Balzani spoke until a few minutes later when a policeman brought Gino in.

Andrea sat on a folding chair against the wall. Balzani indicated that Gino should be seated in one of the chairs next to a metal table. The other policeman, dismissed by the captain, left the room, closing the door behind him.

After a moment, Balzani said, "Miss Perkins, is this one of the men who abducted you and stole the painting from the Accademia?"

"Yes."

How thin and pale he looks, Andrea thought—like a sickly child who had survived one illness only to succumb to another.

"He was there," she added, "but it was the other man who actually forced me into the car."

Gino did not look at her—or at Balzani. He simply sat with his head down, staring at the tabletop.

Pietro would not have been in this predicament, Gino thought. He would have finished the job last night. But Gino could never be like his brother—thank God.

He spread his hands flat on the table and looked at them. Once he had been arrested, the fear was gone. It was all over now. His life was predictable again. In his mind he began to sketch his left hand.

"Your brother was the deceased Pietro Corsini?"

No response.

For a few moments Balzani continued to ask routine questions in a matter-of-fact voice, Gino never answering. Then Balzani sat on the edge of the table. He said nothing for a moment, then jabbed Gino's shoulder hard with his thumb. The arrested man, startled, looked up into Balzani's face.

"You might like to hear exactly what your situation is," Balzani said. "You have been positively identified by Signorina Perkins—so you will be charged. You almost certainly will be convicted, and you could spend the rest of your life in prison."

Gino looked at Andrea for the first time. His face wore a strange expression. Instead of anger or the hatred she might have expected, he looked . . . how? . . . apologetic!

"The charges will be theft and kidnapping," Balzani said. "Kidnapping, in case you didn't know, is a capital offense."

Gino looked down again at his hands and with imaginary charcoal drew the split fingernail of his index finger.

Balzani stood, his arms folded, facing the door for a moment. Then he turned back toward Gino and placed a gentle hand on the young man's shoulder. In the compassionate voice of a priest he said, "I know you were probably forced into being an accomplice by your brother, but the court won't take that into consideration. The court *might*, on the other hand, consider the fact that you have no previous record."

If Balzani expected a reaction, he got none. Suddenly he banged his fist on the table in front of Gino and said in a voice that reverberated against the bare walls of the small room, "You know what happened to your brother! What makes you think his killer won't come after you?"

The man who killed Pietro does not know me . . . he does not know who I am, Gino thought frantically. *But if I am arrested and it is written about in the newspapers . . .*

"Even being in prison won't protect you. There has been more than one man killed in jail. A few thousand lire slipped to someone with a life term . . ." The detective paused to let Gino's imagination complete the sentence.

The prisoner's fingers moved nervously on the tabletop, but still he did not respond. If he refused to talk, wouldn't that prove that he was not a threat to anyone—that he could be trusted?

"I saw Pietro's body in the morgue in Pisa." Balzani's voice was soft again, confiding. "Would you like me to describe the way his face looked?"

Andrea saw Gino shudder. Her own hands were trembling.

"Better still," Balzani pressed the button on the wall intercom. "Sergeant, bring in those pictures of Pietro Corsini that were taken at the morgue . . ."

"No," Gino said, half rising from the chair.

"No," Andrea gasped but neither of the men heard her.

"Never mind," Balzani said, and disengaged the intercom. He slowly walked back to the table. "Now I need you to answer some questions," he said in a dispassionate voice. "If you cooperate . . . if you assist the police in this matter," his tone was confidential again, "I might consider recommending that the kidnapping charge be dropped."

The room was silent. Gino tried to evaluate his situation. If it weren't for the kidnapping charge, jail might not be so bad. They might even let him have his easel and paints. And when he got out he would still have the portrait.

He had to convince the police that he knew nothing about where the portrait of David was hidden. If he told the truth about everything else, they might believe his one lie.

"Isn't it true," Captain Balzani was saying, "that you and your brother, Pietro, with the help of the guard, entered the basement of the Accademia and stole a painting from the safe, that you were interrupted by Miss Perkins and three gentlemen; and that the guard was subsequently shot by your brother in the confusion?"

"No," Gino said.

Balzani looked up from the clipboard he was holding.

"That is not the way it happened," Gino said.

It was exactly as Andrea remembered it. What did he

mean?"

"Let's break it down—one step at a time," Balzani said. "Is it true that with the help of the guard, you and your brother illegally entered the basement of the Accademia?"

"Yes," Gino answered.

"You were interrupted by Miss Perkins and the gentlemen?"

"Yes."

"And hearing a noise inside, the guard came through the basement door to see what had gone wrong—whereupon your brother shot Luca the guard . . ."

"Yes," Gino said, breathing unevenly.

"Then you and your brother took Miss Perkins as a hostage . . ."

"Yes."

". . . and the reason you were there in the basement that night was to steal a painting you believed to be a portrait of David, the work of Michelangelo."

"No," Gino said.

Balzani paused, rubbing the side of his nose. "You did *not* believe it was a painting by Michelangelo?"

"Yes. Oh, yes!" Gino said fervently. "The colors were mixed exactly as he would have done them . . ."

"Then what is the discrepancy in my question?" Balzani said, puzzled.

"We were not there that night to *steal* the portrait," Gino said, looking furtively first at Andrea, then back to Balzani. "We were there to *put it back.*"

Chapter 24

Gino's words came tumbling over each other. He revealed unrelated episodes of life with his brother. He talked with enthusiasm of his classes at the Accademia. He spoke directly to Andrea about the beauty of the portrait of David, complimenting her on the restoration she had done. Balzani let him ramble.

The crux of the story was beginning to emerge. Although Gino lacked the originality to be a great artist, he was, in fact, an expert copyist. His ability had first come to the attention of Leo Fozzi. Fozzi boasted—and it was true—that students from the Accademia competed to have their paintings hung in the lobby of the Albion Hotel where they were for sale on consignment. With an eye for what attracted the attention of the tourists, Fozzi usually selected brightly colored street scenes of Florence and abstractions whose interpretation was left to the viewer and whose popularity depended on the skill of Fozzi's salesmanship.

Several times Gino had approached Fozzi to hang his paintings in the Albion but was always told there was no room available. The hotel proprietor called Gino's landscapes mundane and his still lifes pedestrian. Fozzi advised Gino to go into the black-market business with his brother, Pietro.

After being turned down a fourth time, Gino devised a plan. He checked out a color plate of Modigliani's *Head of a Woman* from the library of the Accademia. Within a few hours he had copied the portrait so exactly that even an expert would have had to subject it to chemical analysis to determine that it was a fake. Of course, an expert would never have considered such a thing because he would have known that the original was a part of the Julian and Joachim J. Aberback collection in New York.

Gino chose Modigliani as the artist he would copy for two reasons. First, the artist's style was so easily recognizable—the pointed chins, the oval eyes, the flaring nostrils, the long swanlike necks. And second, Modigliani had painted in the early 1900s, so there was no need to add the hairline crackle to the surface of the canvas that would have been present on an older painting.

The next day he took his copy to show to Leo Fozzi. Gino's story was that he had accidentally dropped some solvent on a used canvas that he had bought from a warehouse that catered to students. On cleaning the entire canvas, he had discovered, to his great good fortune, the early Modigliani.

"Are you interested in buying it?" Gino had asked Leo Fozzi.

Fozzi pretended to hesitate, but Gino saw the gleam in his eyes and the effort it took for him to keep from jerking it from Gino's hands.

Gino named a price that was many times less than the original would have been worth but demanded to be paid on the spot. Fozzi eagerly accepted, beaming at his new acquisition.

"You think it is a good painting, then?" Gino had asked.

"Good? Yes . . . yes, I think it is good," Fozzi said, smiling to himself at his cleverness and Gino's innocence.

"You consider it good enough to hang beside the others

in the lobby?"

Fozzi looked at him as though Gino's last remark confirmed what he had always suspected—that the young art student was completely demented. "That would be like displaying it on a rack of greeting cards," he said.

And then Gino turned the canvas over and pointed to the manufacturer's mark—that of an art supply company that had been in business only a few years.

At first Fozzi protested that he had been cheated and demanded his money back. But on second thought, and always with an eye for an easy profit, he had said, "My friend, you have talent—a rare talent. With my help you could be the most successful artist in Florence." But Gino had laughed and left with his healthy fee.

Within a week, Fozzi had doubled his investment by selling the fake Modigliani to an unsuspecting tourist as an original. Since then, the hotel proprietor had suggested several times that he and Gino go into business together. But that was not what Gino wanted. One day, he believed, however falsely, he would create a painting that would be admired not only in his lifetime but for centuries to come. A painting that would ultimately find a resting place as prestigious as the Pitti Palace or the Accademia.

He had continued to refuse Fozzi's offers, and instead, worked on his own uninspired paintings. To sharpen his technique, he made copies of masterpieces—literally painting one on top of the other on his used canvases.

When Gino's story showed signs of slowing, Captain Balzani tried to maneuver him back to the question of the fake Michelangelo. He asked, "When was Fozzi first contacted about stealing the portrait of David?"

"The first day after it was brought to the Accademia," Gino said, settling back in his chair now, relaxed and prepared to tell the police captain whatever he wanted to know.

179

"Are you sure?"

"Yes. That's when he called Pietro."

"What exactly did he tell him?"

"I don't know all of it . . . I didn't want to know," Gino said.

Andrea sat forward, listening to Balzani's questions and Gino's answers, mentally filling in her own interpretation where the information was sketchy.

"Fozzi said an American who lived in Florence . . ."

Bud McCauley, Andrea supplied for herself.

". . . called and told him about the portrait and offered to pay Fozzi a great deal of money to have it stolen . . ."

Clint McCauley must have called his nephew immediately after she requested the use of the Mc36 to examine the portrait of David and told Bud to get it for him.

". . . but the American had insisted," Gino said, "that it not be stolen until after it was authenticated."

"Why was that so important?" Balzani asked.

Of course it was important. What value would a painting by Michelangelo have to someone like Clint McCauley unless the world knew of its existence?

"A collector who would buy a masterpiece would want to be sure that it was authentic."

"But you took it before it had been examined," Balzani said. "When?"

"The second night it was in the safe."

"Why?"

"Fozzi remembered my fake Modigliani and saw a way to sell the portrait of David more than once."

"How?"

"He has several wealthy clients who would pay an enormous amount for a stolen Michelangelo . . ."

"You stole the painting the day after it was discovered," Balzani said, making notes on a report form as he talked, "then you painted two copies . . . and the night before

180

the original was to be examined . . . you put it back in the safe . . ."

"But I checked the safe every morning," Andrea said. "The portrait was always there."

"My *copy* was always there," Gino said with a small amount of pride. "I painted it in four hours right there in the basement of the Accademia that first night, then dried it for two hours in the oven in the commissary, wrapped it in cotton batting and put it back in the plastic envelope in the safe."

I never unwrapped it to see . . . I just made sure that the envelope was there every day . . .

"But after you'd made your copy," Balzani said, "why risk taking the original?"

"Fozzi and Pietro were not satisfied with just one copy . . ."

"But couldn't you have used the portrait you painted as a model . . .?"

Gino answered with a sad little laugh. "Fozzi wanted me to work from *photographs*! He wanted me to just take the portrait out of the safe, photograph it, and reproduce it. Can you imagine?" Gino said, looking to Andrea for understanding. "How could I copy the shadings of Michelangelo's colors . . . the depth of the stroke of his brush from the color slide of a Japanese camera?" Gino smiled, shaking his head.

"But what about the Modigliani painting you did to fool Fozzi . . . ?"

Gino's head snapped up at Balzani's words. "I painted that from a professional color plate . . . and only as a joke. And to compare Modigliani . . . a stylistic draftsman, to . . . to . . . Michelangelo . . ." His hands fluttered as he sought an adequate descriptive word. "No, the only way I would consider doing it was if I could use the original as a model for my copies." Again his eyes appealed to Andrea.

"For almost a week . . . I lived with genius. I touched the canvas . . . I marveled at the opalescent quality of his colors . . . I studied the incredible style and composition. Surely, I thought . . . some of this immense talent could be passed on to me . . ." Gino's voice began to quaver, and he stopped and gave an embarrassed cough.

Balzani paused a moment and made notes on the police report to give Gino time to collect his composure.

Andrea looked down at the floor. She could partially understand Gino's overwhelming desire to be a great artist. She had felt much the same way in her early days in college. But she had accepted her limitations and found an area where she could excel. And now she knew that she was the best damned restorer in her field. Poor Gino, why couldn't he be content with being an outstanding copyist? Why couldn't he come to terms with being a mere mortal?

"But I still don't understand," Balzani began again, "how Pietro and Fozzi planned to dispose of the two copies."

"There weren't just two," Gino said.

"How many were there?"

"Eight—completed—and I had the background painted on the ninth."

"Eight?" Andrea asked, sure that she hadn't heard him correctly. "You painted eight? All as good as the two I saw?"

Gino nodded. "The sixth one is actually the best," he said, and for the first time there was real pride in his voice.

"Where are the others?" Balzani shook his head in wonder.

"In my uncle's warehouse in the Pisa marina. That's where I worked. The light wasn't as good as in the Accademia, but it was adaquate. The copy that the policemen found on the boat was a gift of appreciation for the use of the warehouse." Gino grinned at Andrea, knowing she would appreciate the irony. "It was like Michelangelo giving the portrait to his patron, Lorenzo de' Medici. . ."

"How did Fozzi and Pietro plan to dispose of eight—" Balzani started.

"Nine. I would have finished the other one . . ."

"Nine . . . portraits of David. How did they plan to pass them all off as originals and not be discovered?"

"That's why it was important to have the original authenticated before it was stolen. The collectors would know they were buying stolen merchandise and weren't likely to advertise the fact."

"But would there have been time for the Accademia to make a formal announcement if you planned to steal it the night after?"

"Fozzi thought of that," Gino said. "He knew my copies wouldn't be worth very much unless the buyers already knew about the discovery . . . and the theft."

"And how did he plan to handle it?" Balzani asked with growing admiration for the strategy.

"He thought surely the story of a masterpiece that had been discovered and immediately stolen would somehow be leaked to the press. But—just in case—he took his own photographs of the portrait. Fozzi was going to send them and his story anonymously to *La Nazione*."

"And the newspaper would then question Vittorio Sassetti about it," Balzani added.

"Yes."

The police captain paused a moment, then turned to Andrea with the next question. "If Sassetti were asked about the painting, would he have denied it?"

"No," she said. "He might not have volunteered the information about a stolen Michelangelo. But if he were questioned he would not deny it."

"Fozzi seems to have thought of everything," Balzani sighed and sat on the edge of the table. "Except . . .

wouldn't a collector want to have such an expensive paint-ing authenticated for himself?" and he went on to answer his own question: "No, probably not. He had knowingly bought a stolen painting, and as far as he knew, it had already been checked out on the most sophisticated com-puter in existence. But let's say someone *did* discover he had been cheated and came back to Fozzi with the infor-mation . . ."

"Fozzi would have refunded his money," Gino said casually. "He would have said that he and Pietro sold the portrait in good faith, that they had believed it was genuine—but they would gladly refund the customer's money. If only five of the nine sales held up, they would still have more money than they had ever dreamed of having."

"And if the buyer was still unhappy," Balzani laughed, "where was he going to go to complain?"

Andrea noticed how exhausted Gino looked as he propped his elbows on the metal table in the interrogation room and let his head drop into his hands. To give him a moment's rest, she turned and talked quietly to Balzani. "Theirs was even a better scheme than the fake *Mona Lisa*."

"A fake *Mona Lisa*?"

"There again, there was more than one."

"But it's hanging on the wall in the Louvre. How could anyone believe . . ."

"It was stolen in 1911. An Italian workman simply cut it from the frame, tucked it under his coat and ambled out with it. It was found two years later here in Florence in the workman's trunk, and returned to Paris. But in the mean-time, several copies had been made and sold. And ever since then, from time to time, some enterprising con artist will come up with a convincing story that the picture now hanging in the Louvre is a copy and he owns the genuine article. I even heard of one wealthy collector who was approached with the notion of buying it, then donating it to the National Gallery in Washington. The would-be seller pointed out that he would earn the gratitude of the nation—and considerable tax deductions."

"It sounds as though you deal with almost as many criminals in your job as I do in mine," Balzani said, and touched Gino lightly on the shoulder. "One thing I can't understand, Gino, is why you came back to the Accademia this morning. You must have known we'd be looking for you there."

Gino did not own a watch, he told Captain Balzani and Andrea, and the clock on the dashboard of Pietro's car had not worked since he owned it. He told them of spending the night waiting for Leo Fozzi in the garage of the Albion Hotel. He had no idea of the time until he asked the bakeryman who had greeted him earlier.

"A quarter of seven," the man said. Having made his delivery at the hotel kitchen he banged the double metal doors of the truck closed and climbed up into the driver's seat. "You must have had a hell of a good time last night," the man said, "to look as sick as you do this morning." He waved and laughed and drove away.

Gino had thirty minutes to wait. Fozzi was always in the garage warehouse by 7:15. Punctuality was one of the hotel proprietor's few virtues. But Gino wasn't sure Fozzi was even in the hotel. He had seen him leave with a man in a black Ferrari.

Of course they could have returned and Fozzi could have gotten out at the front entrance, where Gino would not have seen him.

He got back in Pietro's car, slumped down and laid his head against the back of the seat. His stomach still felt delicate—rolling and pitching—as it had on his uncle's boat. As he waited, his breathing steadied and the nausea left. He may even have dozed until he heard angry voices at the hotel's service entrance.

"I'm not supposed to leave these artichokes unless he pays in advance!" an angry voice said.

Gino roused himself to look out and see a man standing in the back of a flatbed truck surrounded by straw baskets of vegetables. A cook in a white apron and cap who stood in the doorway shrugged, and said, "Sorry, signore, he is always here at this time." The cook shrugged again and turned to go inside. "He must be sick."

But it was Gino who was sick. He couldn't chance going into the hotel to find Fozzi. There was no choice now. He had to get to Naples the best way he could. But he had no money. He could not even buy gasoline for the long trip.

Where would he get the money? Was there someone he could borrow it from? That, he decided, was what he should do; borrow money from a friend.

Then, even though he knew it was dangerous, he had gone to visit with his classmates at the Accademia.

Balzani had made notes of Gino's story, and when it was concluded, he waited a moment and then said, "Gino, there is still one very important thing you haven't told us."

"I've told you everything."

"You haven't told us where the original portrait of David is now."

"I don't know," Gino said. And this was his one lie. Gino kept his head down as he spoke, afraid to look at Andrea, afraid his eyes would give him away. He studied the lower half of the door to the hallway; zinc white, ivory black, equal parts, with a touch of yellow ocher. The portrait was safe where he had hidden it.

"You *do* know, don't you? Pietro must have told you." Balzani sat in a chair opposite Gino, watching him intently.

"All I know is that it is somewhere no one would think to look for a work of art," Gino said with a small sardonic smile, and quickly added, "That is all Pietro told me."

Captain Balzani studied the young man for a moment longer, then said, "I think it's time we brought Leo Fozzi in and heard his story, too." He crossed to the intercom and spoke to the desk sergeant.

"Yes, sir?" a voice hardly audible through the static answered the buzz.

"Send someone to the Albion Hotel and pick up Leo Fozzi for questioning."

"Leo Fozzi is already here, sir," the voice came back.

"Oh?" Balzani said, surprised. "Then bring him in."

"No, sir . . . he *is* here . . . but in the morgue," the desk sergeant said. "They fished him out of the Arno about an hour ago."

Suddenly there was a soft, piercing sound that might have come from the intercom. Andrea thought at first that it had. It started on a high-pitched sustained note that trailed down and broke into rhythmic sobs. Gino lifted his head then threw it back so that the cry choked in his throat and was reduced to a clicking noise.

All the tragedies of his life confronted him at once. Like armored horsemen—swords drawn, one by one they attacked him. The first blow was to have had such an unloving brother. The second, to have witnessed his brother killing his friend. A third devastation, to have lost his brother whom he hated, but on whom he depended. And now his one hope, Leo Fozzi, had been killed, too. Gino threw one arm across his face and wiped his eyes with his sleeve. But the strongest opponent of all—the one he could not defend against—stood revealed for the first time. The greatest sadness of his life was to have been given such skill without talent.

His eyes were still covered with one arm; the other arm

lay limp on the table, palm up. Suddenly Gino felt something soft in his hand and someone's fingers lightly squeezing his. He looked down and saw a wad of pink tissue and the signorina's hand. He could not meet her eyes, but he responded to her kindness with a slight pressure of his curling fingers.

Andrea sat back in the folding chair again, her eyes on the worn linoleum.

Balzani was still at the intercom, hearing the details of Fozzi's death and only marginally aware of Gino's condition until he completed listening to the report. Then he touched Andrea on the shoulder and said softly, "Come out into the hall." Outside, he said, "I'm sorry to have put you through this. You may as well leave. I don't think Gino will be able to tell us anything else. Not now, at least."

"He's so pathetic. Do you think he knows where the portrait of David is?"

"Of course he does. He's not a very accomplished liar. We'll find out. But I think it's useless to try to talk with him anymore now."

"Oh, no," Andrea agreed sincerely. "I'll go on to the Accademia, then. Call me if I can be of help."

"You can be sure of it . . . whether you can be of help or not." He leaned down and kissed her lightly on the cheek, clasped her hand a moment, then went back to the interrogation room to take Gino Corsini back to his cell.

Chapter 25

The dashboard computer in the limousine blinked through a dozen small windows in digital accuracy that told the miles-per-hour, gallons-per-mile, revolutions-per-minute, time-to-the-second, interior temperature, distance-of-vehicle-ahead, distance-of-vehicle-behind, and the one Bud McCauley looked down to check, the telephone range.

Seeing that he was inside the limits, he called the Albion Hotel. When the call was answered, he asked for "Signorina Andrea Perkins, *per favore*."

"She is not in, signore."

Bud would have hung up if she had been there. "Do you know where I might be able to reach her?"

"No, signore, perhaps the Galleria dell'Accademia . . ."

Bud replaced the telephone under the dashboard. He turned on Via Ricasoli, and in a few blocks, drove past the Accademia, around the corner, and parked in a public parking lot. Reaching into the glove compartment he took out a pair of dark glasses and a white tennis hat which he put on, turning down the brim all the way around. Last, he opened a small leather case and took out a metal cylinder—a silencer—and attached it to the gun he was wearing in a holster beneath his arm.

That morning at the airport in Pisa, Tom Daley had hurried to board the private jet. But Clint McCauley had stayed behind several minutes to talk with his nephew. "That Perkins girl knows where the portrait of David is," he had said. Then he slapped the car door next to Bud and added, "I want it."

Bud knew Clint McCauley had not just expressed a desire—he had given a command. But what his uncle did not know was that Bud had no intention of obeying it.

Death, danger, and great deeds . . . Yes, Bud felt *revised and rejuvenated.*

He left the car, hoping to find a group of tourists visiting the Accademia that he could blend in with. It would not hurt to know the layout of the building if this was where Andrea Perkins spent most of her time.

At first he had just been angry at his uncle's reprimand, but the anger had hardened into determination. And on the drive back from Pisa to Florence Bud had devised a plan that would prove to Clint McCauley that for once, he had misjudged his nephew.

"I'm disappointed," McCauley had said, "real disappointed in the way you handled gettin' the picture for me."

Bud had not answered.

"I was plannin' on bringin' you back to Texas with me." McCauley always slipped into his Texas-rancher accent when he wanted something from his nephew. "You still want to go back to Texas, don'cha, Bud?"

"Yes, sir."

"I can probably get that arrest warrant handled for you," Clint McCauley said, adding quickly, "and I will . . . when I think you're ready to take care of things back home for me."

Bud had felt anger flash through his body, making the back of his neck feel hot; turning it red. He knew what

Clint McCauley meant. If Bud got the portrait of David for him, he would allow his nephew to take orders from him in Houston instead of Italy.

The first year Bud McCauley had been in Italy, where his uncle had sent him after he had shot the man in a barroom, he had begged his uncle to fix it so that he could go back. But he had been in Italy two years now, and Texas seemed farther and farther away. He was ready for new *danger and great deeds*.

Walking along the sidewalk across the street from the Accademia, Bud kept under the awnings of the buildings, distancing himself from the street where the driver of a passing car might recognize him.

When he reached the back of the Accademia, he cut through the parking lot, noting that the space where Andrea Perkins' name was stenciled on the curb was vacant. Good. He wanted a chance to familiarize himself with the building before confronting her.

At the corner, he turned toward the entrance, walking up the marble steps, surprised to see there were no other people around. He had almost reached the double doors of the entry before he noticed the sign: CLOSED MONDAY.

Fighting back his anger at the unexpected, he stood a moment revising his plan. Then he noticed a restaurant across the street where umbrella-topped tables sat on the sidewalk and provided a view of both the front entrance and the parking lot. He crossed and selected a spot where he could see, but not easily be seen.

He ordered a locally brewed beer. Even though the Accademia was closed, he thought she still might come. She had a key. She wasn't at the hotel. Maybe she was on her way here now. He decided to wait for a while.

Holding the frosted glass at an angle, he poured slowly from the amber bottle to lessen the foam. If the painting was so important to Clint McCauley, and if he was willing to pay so generously for it, there must be others. There must be other wealthy art collectors who would be just as willing. It might take some time to ferret them out, but he would have time.

Madrid should be full of wealthy patrons of the Prado who would pay generously for a painting by Michelangelo.

Bud McCauley took a sip of beer and stretched his legs under the table, crossing his cowboy boots at the ankle. Spain—yes, he would like Spain. He smiled to himself as he thought of bullfights . . . flamenco dancers . . . *death, danger, and great deeds.*

Chapter 26

The morning had withdrawn its promise of sunshine. Rain, sparse and tentative so far, fell from a dark sky that threatened a torrent. Andrea ran from the back door of the police station to the parking lot, holding her handbag over her head as a makeshift umbrella.

She quickly climbed inside her red Alfa Romeo, shutting out the rain but not the cold. The dense, dark clouds gave the city an eerie quality, as though the world had plunged forward and spun ahead into evening, even though the dashboard clock said it was not quite noon.

Andrea drove onto Via Nazionale. Dense fog from the Arno filled the space between the street and the low-hanging storm clouds, making driving treacherous. As traffic inched along the slippery streets, Andrea thought about Gino's story. It was an incredible plan that would have worked if it hadn't been for the foolish argument between Tom Daley and Vittorio that night at McCauley's villa, if Vittorio hadn't been determined to prove that the painting bore the Medici Medallion and not a merchant's price tag, as Daley had suggested.

She turned right onto Via Guelfa. Other parts of Gino's story chased each other through her head. If, as Aldo Balzani said, Gino *did* know where the portrait was . . . where would that be? It didn't seem likely that he would entrust a masterpiece that he revered to his oafish brother, Pietro. Gino would have made sure that it was safe. "Somewhere no one would think to look for a work of art," he had said, and from his tone of voice and the sad, helpless look on his face when he said it, Andrea believed that was true. He *must* have had it with him when he waited for Fozzi in the garage. Gino was on his way to Naples if he could get the money from the hotel proprietor. But then when Fozzi didn't show up . . . My God! she thought suddenly, *that's* where it must be! He hid it in one of the storerooms in the garage!

She considered passing a lumbering panel truck ahead in her hurry to get to the Albion Hotel. But, no, she thought with a sinking feeling, Gino would not have left the portrait of David there. He would not have exposed it to the dampness and the rats that infested the basement.

Ahead was Via Ricasoli. She drove through the intersection, past the austere high stone wall of the Accademia, which had taken on a peculiar look of villainy in the uncommon midday darkness. Skidding slightly on a sharp turn, she steered her car into her reserved parking spot in the lot behind the building. Why had Gino come back to the Accademia this morning when he knew it was so dangerous? To borrow money from a friend, he had said. Then suddenly she knew why he had been there. She knew exactly where Gino would think no one would look for a work of art.

Across the street, Bud McCauley was the only customer still seated outside at an umbrella table of the sidewalk café where he had been waiting.

Through the fog, it was hard to distinguish the lines of the automobile that had just entered the parking lot, but he knew whose name was stenciled on the curb in front of where it had parked. Dropping a freshly lit cigarette on the wet concrete, he hurried toward the Accademia and anonymously joined a group of fifteen or twenty students who stood companionably huddled under the narrow overhang outside the basement door waiting for the bus that would take them home from their last class of the day.

Andrea, head down against the beginning rain, locked her car and entered the basement. She wove her way through the straggling students who were still milling about, putting away their equipment, pushing their wheeled easels into the storage room. She wished they would hurry. She was impatient to see if she had guessed right about Gino.

Above the noise of the students' chatter was the sound of a radio in the security office. Andrea had a momentary start as she remembered the guard, Luca, and his passion for the same rock music.

Of course, Andrea realized, Vittorio would have had to hire someone new. She decided to introduce herself. His office would be a place to wait until the basement was empty.

The blaring music made conversation impossible, and it was still distracting after the guard turned it down. She told him she was the assistant curator of the Accademia. As they exchanged names and handshakes she stood with her back to the workroom.

Outside, Bud McCauley watched through the open door to the alley and chose that moment to enter the building. With the thoughtful frown of one who had re-turned for a forgotten object, he walked unnoticed past the few remaining students, past Andrea and the guard, to the back of the room and stood in the shadows beneath the stairway out of sight.

Presently the outside door banged shut as the last fledg-ling artist left. Andrea stepped aside so the new guard could lock up. He took a key ring from a loop on his belt, double-locked the door and bolted it, then went back to his office to abuse his ears once more with the loud music.

Believing that she was alone now, Andrea went quickly to the storage room where the students' tripod easels stood. They looked like a community of skeletal A-frames on wheels. On top of the filing cabinet stood a small marble bust of Cosimo de' Medici by an early unknown sculptor. Glancing at some of the canvases still drying on the easels, Andrea saw that this bust had been the model for today's lesson.

She pushed it to one side and reached for a gooseneck lamp behind it. She turned the lamp on and angled it toward the far wall. Each student's name was stenciled on the back of his easel. Andrea read them one by one and pushed them impatiently aside, going deeper into the room.

Bud McCauley crept closer to the storage area to see what she was doing and also to make sure there was no other exit. There wasn't. He returned to his station under the stairway to the first floor, and waited.

At last Andrea found what she was looking for—the easel bearing Gino Corsini's name.

Poor Gino, Andrea thought; poor sad, unimaginative, lonely Gino. Was his own easel the one place he thought no one would look for a work of art?

She was almost reluctant to lift the flap covering the canvas. Then, carefully, she folded back the coarse cloth that was attached to the top of the easel. There, as Gino had unwittingly told her it would be, was the portrait of David.

It was just as Andrea had seen it last in her office; the vivid blue eyes, the deep, gleaming bronze hair that curled around the face painted in perfect flesh tones, the full mouth set in determination, but with no trace of fear of the

Philistine giant he was soon to conquer. In the top corner of the painting was the medallion of the Medici, the sword and swan under the arches of the letter M. In the lower-right-hand corner was the signature she had uncovered: Michelangelo Buonarroti.

But the most telling thing for Andrea was the one blemish that identified this as the original instead of one of Gino's excellent copies. It was the smudge of glue left on the wooden frame when the canvas had been transferred to a stronger backing. The brownish blob was exactly as she had seen it when she had first begun to clean the painting.

Andrea carefully lifted the portrait from the easel and went back into the basement room, pausing in the better light to look at it again. Then she rang for the elevator and heard the door clang shut on the floor above.

Slow as it was, the elevator might have been faster than the stairs, but she could not bear to stand and wait for it. She felt a sudden urgency to get the painting safely locked away, and to call Aldo Balzani and tell him of her discovery.

Bud McCauley knew what she was holding. He watched her cross the room, heard the click of her high-heeled shoes on the stairs above him, heard her slide the bolt on the door above.

Bud McCauley did not follow. He leaned against the wall and reached under his arm, caressing the holster of his gun as he often did in thoughtful moments. There was no rush. She wasn't going anywhere, and he had another matter to attend to first. There could be no mistakes this time.

Hardly more than a minute later, when he followed Andrea up the stairs, he said softly to himself, "Tacrong, carong . . ."

*   *   *

The first thing Aldo Balzani did after reading the official report of Leo Fozzi's death was to check with the Department of Vehicle Registration. As he suspected, there was a black Ferrari registered to Clint McCauley.

The second thing he did was send a police car to bring Bud McCauley in for questioning. At last he had something to go on—he had an eyewitness. Gino Corsini had seen Fozzi leave the basement of the Albion Hotel with a man he could identify. The police captain was all but certain that man was Bud McCauley.

The phone on Balzani's desk rang. He answered. "Yes?"

"Captain," the desk sergeant said, "car seventeen just radioed in from Clint McCauley's villa."

"Yes?"

"There is no one there."

"What do you mean?"

"The butler or somebody told them that Bud McCauley left about four hours ago to drive his uncle and another American to the airport in Pisa and hasn't come back yet. What are the orders?"

"Tell the men to stay there until he returns or until they hear from me again."

Balzani disconnected the call and immediately dialed the number of the Accademia. He had to warn Andrea. As long as Bud McCauley's whereabouts were unknown, she could be in danger. A feeling of dread spread through him, sickening and debilitating. He tried to comfort himself with the thought that she was in a public building where swarms of visitors would be. But the memory of Pietro Corsini's death—shot in a crowd by the Tower of Pisa made him even more uneasy. He had not realized until this moment how monumentally important Andrea Perkins' well-being was to him.

On the third ring he got the recorded message that the

Galleria dell'Accademia was closed this afternoon but that the caller was invited to visit tomorrow morning at ten.

"God! She's probably in her office alone!"

He ran from the building not bothering to stop for his raincoat, and had the siren turned on in his car before he was out of the parking lot.

Chapter 27

On the first floor of the Accademia, the sound of rain was more pronounced than it had been in the basement. There was nothing tentative about it now. Though not a downpour, it was steady and determined. Andrea closed the door behind her at the head of the stairs and entered the apse where the statue of David stood. As she held the painting of David, she looked up at the face she had examined every day when she entered the Accademia and imagined that his expression seemed pleased that the other David had been returned.

Words from the Book of Samuel seemed to ring from the walls of the great hall.

. . . *he was ruddy, and withal of beautiful countenance, and goodly to look to.*

As she started through the great exhibition hallway toward her office, everything her eyes fell upon was of exquisite beauty; the magnificent Flemish tapestries . . . the dozen golden ormolu chairs with the red velvet upholstery that were spaced along the wall between the six full-scale Michelangelo statues flanking the room.

The rain had begun in earnest. Andrea could hear it pounding outside, an amplified percussion to the brassy music of the guard's radio.

And there was another familiar sound, but out of context with the serenity of the deserted gallery. The doorway at the top of the basement stairs opened and closed.

Andrea felt uneasy. Her shoulder-strap bag slapped against her hip as she turned quickly to see who was there. She saw no one. She began to walk faster as she approached the foyer.

She wouldn't relax, she told herself, until the portrait was locked inside the vault.

She smiled to herself at the irony. McCauley's Mc36 was still in the basement, crated and scheduled to be shipped back to Houston. But she planned to use it first. She and Vittorio could invite the curators from the Pitti Palace and the Museo Nazionale to witness and confirm their findings.

Did she hear footsteps? A clicking noise—heel taps? Again she looked behind her. Again she saw no one. Had someone followed her and hidden behind one of the statues? Some of the darker words from the Book of Samuel sprang into her mind: *Yet a man is risen to pursue thee, and to seek thy soul* . . .

Andrea hurried on. *Get to your office. Lock the door.*

Through an angled window in the foyer she could see a heavy sheet of rain that fell from the darkened sky. She could see her own reflection, her face pale, her eyes wide and troubled. And behind the image, she could see another reflection. A man crept out from behind the statue of Saint Matthew. She recognized him. It was Bud McCauley. Why was he here? In the split second before she turned to confront him, she saw in the mirrored window his hand reach beneath his jacket to the holster under his arm and pull out a gun.

Andrea ran the few remaining steps that took her into the foyer out of sight. She had three choices. She could try to hide in the first gallery . . . the second gallery . . . or the ticket booth near the front door. But there was no place to hide the painting in either of the galleries—so she ducked into the booth. Terrified, she crouched in the corner.

She knew exactly why Bud McCauley was here. Soundlessly, she leaned the portrait of David against the inside wall.

He was in the foyer now, inches from her. She could have reached through the open door and touched his blue denim trousers. He stood there calmly, the gun in his hand. Almost casually he entered the first gallery to look for her.

Andrea slipped the leather bag from her shoulder. She unbuckled her sandals and eased them off. Should she try to make it to the stairs and find the guard on the second floor?

At that moment she heard an aimless, tuneless whistling in the upstairs hallway as the guard came toward the head of the stairs. Was there time to warn him? No. Bud must have heard him, too; his steps were returning. Wait. Wait until the guard was at the top of the stairs. Then yell—and hope he had good reflexes!

The whistling had stopped. Bud moved toward the stairs. The guard stood at the top of the railing. Andrea started to call out, but then she heard a whistle. Not the bored lonely whistle she had heard before. It was the sputtering, whistling sound of the silencer on Bud McCauley's gun.

The guard's feet lifted from the floor and his body twisted, then crumpled and fell forward, rolling headfirst like an accomplished acrobat. The momentum slowed halfway, and he lay sprawled, face up, spread-eagled on the stairs. Blood from the hole in his chest ran down on the step beside him and dripped to the one below.

Bud McCauley climbed the stairs and bent over the guard's body to make sure, Andrea guessed, that he was dead.

In the brief time that his back was turned, Andrea darted from the ticket booth and through the first gallery toward the back stairs. She moved soundlessly in her stockinged feet across the marble floor.

The music from the downstairs radio drowned out the sound of the rain. Andrea slid the bolt on the inside of the door, then ran down the stairs, yelling to the guard. Why didn't he answer? She continued to yell until she reached his office.

When she saw what was inside, she had to brace herself with both hands against the jamb.

The radio was lying on the floor in a pool of blood. The guard slumped over the desk. His head rested on one of his outstretched arms. The back of his skull was gone. A partly congealed mass of red and gray matter had seeped down his neck and puddled on the desk top. Bud had shot him before he followed Andrea from the basement.

She knew Bud would hear her yelling, but she had risked it. And now she heard the latch on the door upstairs being turned. She forced herself to reach around the body of the guard for his holster. The gun was gone. So were his keys.

Quickly Andrea switched off the lamp on the desk and the lights in the basement. It was almost pitch-black. Darkness would be her ally. She knew the Accademia— Bud McCauley didn't. He kicked at the door.

Andrea ran to the storage room and pushed a dozen or more easels out into the work area. They might slow him down in the dark—or at least let her know where he was. With one of them, she propped open the door to the elevator. Again there was the sound of a boot against the door—and now the splintering of wood.

The wheels of the easels skidded across the floor. They banged against the tables and the walls. They should provide some hazard. Bud's eye wouldn't be accustomed to the dark.

Again the boot cracked against the surrendering door that bounced open and banged against the wall.

Bud McCauley stood silhouetted in the doorway above, his gun held down at his side. "There's only you and me," he said. "There won't be anyone else here till morning."

Slowly he started down the stairs, feeling his way with his hand against the wall.

Andrea was still in the doorway of the storage room. She put her hand on top of the filing cabinet beside her. She felt with slow, careful circles that advanced until she touched the base of the marble Cosimo de' Medici bust. Gripping it by the neck, she crept into the elevator.

"Have you ever been to Spain?" Bud's voice was coming from near the back door. "I'll take you with me. I've been collecting Uncle Clint's castoffs for years." Bud's brittle laughter grated against the music that still came from the persistent radio on the floor of the security office.

In the elevator, Andrea found the button for the first floor. Wait, she cautioned herself. Wait until he is as far away from the stairs as possible.

"You might even like me better than him. I'm pretty damn good . . ." An easel crashed to the floor. "Son of a bitch," Bud muttered.

"I'll eventually find the light switch, you know," he said, rubbing his hand slowly up and down the wall as he moved farther from the stairs.

He *would* find it. As soon as he reached the security office and felt inside the door.

Now! Andrea shoved the easel out of the elevator with all her strength. It crashed into others, toppling some, sending wet canvases skidding across the floor. She pushed the elevator button. The motor started.

Bud spun toward the sound. He started toward it. His foot caught in the crosspiece of an upended easel. He tripped, dropping to his knees.

Grindingly, painfully slowly, the elevator was moving. Even in the dark, the metal cage gave Andrea no protection.

She heard the whistling sound she had heard before in the foyer. A bullet clanged against a metal crosspiece of the elevator's cage. *Thank God it was too dark for him to aim carefully.* There was the sound of the gun again. This time she felt the impact, then a stinging sensation in her upraised arm. The bullet had hit the underside, missing the bone. It cut cleanly through her flesh and continued its upward trajectory, pinging against the wall and bouncing to the floor.

Andrea dropped her arm to her side. It began to throb and she could feel a soggy stickiness spreading in the sleeve of her sweater.

The elevator labored by inches. Another bullet hit the brick wall of the shaft beneath her.

Bud started for the stairs. More easels clattered to the floor. Andrea heard him cursing and the sound of wood flung against the wall.

Now she was waist-level with the first floor. There was a distant rumble of thunder and a sudden flash of lightning reflected softly on the white marble of the hallway. Should she try to get to her office? Lock herself in and barricade the door? With only one arm she knew she couldn't.

The elevator jerked to a stop. Still clutching the bust of Cosimo de' Medici in her right hand, she pushed the grillwork door open with her elbow and stepped out. Her foot touched something warm and slippery on the cold white marble floor. When she looked down she saw that it was her own blood.

Bud McCauley was on the stairway. Desperately she reached inside the elevator, pressing the button to send it to the top floor. It might distract him long enough for her to retrieve her keys from the ticket booth and get out the front door.

Oh God! She was leaving a trail! There were drops of blood like red confetti behind her as she ran.

The stairway door crashed open. There was no time left. All she could do was double back into the great hall.

The agony, the turmoil and anguish of the six Michelangelo statues confronted her. And David, in the apse at the other end, stood eternally on the brink of battle.

All their conflicts were frozen in time.

Hers was approaching closer by the second.

Bud McCauley was in the next gallery. She heard his footsteps. Then they stopped—now to look behind a Florentine sofa—now behind a display table—soon here behind the statues themselves.

Andrea pushed an ormolu chair with her knee next to one of the *Prisoner* sculptures. She climbed on the chair, then to the pedestal; gently pushing the chair back toward the wall out of sight with her foot. She leaned against the statue, trying to become a part of it. Wishing she could climb into the marble the sculpted Prisoner had tried for centuries to escape.

The footsteps continued, softer, then louder, checking both galleries, not hurrying, knowing he would find her. And still she could hear the incessant rain, the faint tinkling of the basement radio, and above all, ringing in her ears, the ominous words of Samuel!

I have rewarded thee with evil!

"So you're in here." He stood in the arched doorway laughing. "I see I clipped you even in the dark. Looks like you've lost quite a bit of blood." He circled the *Palestrina Pietà*. "You haven't long now, you know . . . there are only five more statues."

Two—there were only two between her and Bud.

There is but a step between me and death . . .

Her left arm throbbed against her rib cage. Her legs felt weak, in danger of buckling. She concentrated all her energy on her upraised right hand, gripping the Medici bust so tightly her fingers were numb.

Bud was only a few feet away, looking down at the floor, expecting to see her feet, expecting her to be on the back side of the statue toward the wall.

. . . took thence a stone and slung it and smote the Philistine in the forehead . . .

Andrea's intake of breath made Bud McCauley look up. But before he could react, she slung her arm down with strength she had never had before. The corner of the bust crashed into Bud McCauley's forehead. It sliced through the skin, and she thought she heard the cracking of bone.

The stone sunk into his forehead and he fell upon his face . . .

Bud McCauley fell to his knees, still staring up at her, unbelieving. The skin of his forehead above an eye lay open, strangely bloodless at first as though a wedge had been neatly cut from it. And then the blood seeped through and down into his eye as he fell forward on the marble floor. His arms stretched in front of him and the gun clattered and skidded across the floor's smooth surface, then banged against the wall and disappeared in the darkness somewhere behind an imperturbable statue.

Was he dead? She could not tell if he was alive or dead. She stared at the back of his jacket, watching for the rise and fall of breathing, but saw no movement.

Easing her legs forward, she held her injured arm close to her side and jumped the two feet to the floor.

His face looked lifeless, but the blood continued to

flow. She could not take her eyes off the gash in his forehead. She should have been watching his hands. Suddenly he gripped one of her ankles. She screamed and tried to kick free.

His hand had the strength of rigor mortis. She felt chained to a dead man, trying to walk, trying to free herself, his body trailing after her, sliding easily on the slick surface. But then his grip weakened and she freed herself. Running toward the foyer, she looked back to see him bracing himself with his hands, pulling his body up on all fours.

At the stairs, she stopped to scavenge the body of the dead guard for a weapon. His gun lay beside him, partly hidden by the disarray of his jacket. She grabbed it, then ran to the second floor, pausing at the railing at the top to look back as Bud McCauley, staggering from the blow, turned his dazed face up at her.

She couldn't hold the gun steady with just one hand. She braced it on the railing and pulled the trigger. There was a click. Only that.

Bud McCauley laughed, his face a bloody macabre mask, as he reached into the pocket of his jacket and held up a handful of bullets for Andrea to see. He threw them in the air and they clattered, rolled and scattered on the floor as he came toward the stairway.

Andrea turned and ran down the second-floor hall. The elevator! Would she be safer in the basement? No. Without her keys there was no way out.

She slid open the outer grillwork door of the elevator, pushing it all the way back to the wall with her shoulder and securing it by a metal catch with her good hand. Then, opening the cage enough to get her hand in, she pressed the button marked "B" and closed the door so the motor would start.

The cables creaked and moaned and the motor laboriously bore the empty elevator toward the lower floors. Maybe Bud McCauley would be fooled this time.

She picked up the empty gun from the floor where she had put it and searched frantically for a place to hide.

A few feet behind her was a brocade screen folded halfway open like an accordion that stood on lacquered legs. She jumped behind it and waited. At last she heard a metallic groan and the elevator stopped. Now there was only the rain that beat against the roof . . . only the rain and then the slow sound of metal heel taps on the stairs.

He had not been fooled.

The slow, deliberate steps were coming nearer. She looked down and could see his feet in the twelve-inch space between the floor and the bottom of the screen. If he looked down, he could see hers, too!

"Game's over," he said. The screen tilted as he grabbed it on each side.

The gun was useless, even to hit him with. She couldn't reach him over the top of the screen. Instead, she took a step backward, hunched over, lurched forward and hit Bud McCauley in the chest with her head. He reeled backward.

She heard a surprised gasp. The screen clattered to the floor. The gasp became a scream. It was strangely high-pitched and seemingly endless, trailing off, traveling down to the center of the earth . . . to the bottom of the elevator shaft.

There was a muffled thud as Bud McCauley's body hit the roof of the elevator two floors below and lay still, the bloody head at a grotesque angle that would not have been possible if his neck had not been broken.

Andrea did not hear the siren. She did not hear the pounding on the front door. She did not hear the ancient oak splinter away from the lock and crash against the inside wall, or the running feet that took the stairs two at a time. The first sound her mind would accept or acknowledge were the whispered words of Aldo Balzani as he held her close against him. "Andrea . . . darlin' . . . it's all right, it's all right."

Chapter 28

Arnolfo Becocci, representing the Pitti Palace, and Carlo Ruggeri, from the Museo Nazionale, sat uncomfortably in folding metal chairs outside the small X-ray cubicle of the Galleria dell'Accademia as Vittorio Sassetti expansively explained the coded information garnered by the Mc36 computer.

The Mc36 had confirmed everything Andrea had discovered the first time she examined the portrait of David. The undercoating was laid on exactly as it was in the Doni tondo, for centuries the only known easel painting by Michelangelo. The length of the artist's stroke corresponded in the same way. The pigment was suspended in egg yolk, as should have been the case. The Medici Medallion, which had been the computer's first consideration, was found to be authentic. The perforations in the canvas that formed the design of a swan and a sword in the arches of the letter *M* matched exactly the original metal seal that was on loan to the Accademia from the Medici Palace. By virtue of the medallion alone the experts were satisfied that the portrait of David had been a favored painting belonging to the Medici.

Andrea's original examination could date the canvas only to within five years. The computer was exact. The portrait was painted in 1495. This information began the first argument among the three curators.

"But Vittorio, you believed the portrait to be a gift from Michelangelo to Lorenzo de' Medici . . . a tribute for his patronage . . ." Carlo Ruggeri said.

"I had thought so," Vittorio said defensively, knowing what one of the other two men would undoubtedly point out next. "But that was merely my own speculation . . ."

"No, it was a sound assumption—the same one I would have made," Arnolfo Becocci said, "except that Lorenzo had been dead for three years in 1495."

"And Piero de' Medici was in exile in Venice," Carlo Ruggeri added.

"So to whom might Michelangelo have given it?" Arnolfo Becocci asked.

The three men continued to discuss the Medici family and Michelangelo as though gossiping about contemporary mutual acquaintances. The curator of the Pitti Palace pointed out that Piero de' Medici, who came to power after the death of his father, Lorenzo, was inept as a leader, hated by the Florentines and driven into exile by the religious fanatic Savonarola after having ruled the city for only two years.

"And Michelangelo hated Piero," the curator of the Museo Nazionale added, glancing around the room as though he feared one of the Medicis or Michelangelo himself might overhear what they were discussing.

"Oh, yes! Hated him! Avoided him at all costs when he lived in the palace with Lorenzo," the curator from the Pitti Palace agreed.

"One does wonder why he would give such a gift to Piero, a man no longer in power, a man he hated," Vittorio Sassetti conceded.

The discussion continued but was dropped and forgotten when the Mc36 began to print out the results of the analysis of the signature. The distance between the letters was measured, recorded and compared with a known original, as was the pressure applied to the brush by the artist.

The results appeared on the small cathode ray tube, and were also printed out on paper tape. The word *discrepancy* appeared above two columns of digits that did not match.

In words—translated from the computer's numbers— the portrait was indeed a fifteenth century work but not by Michelangelo; it was a forgery.

Epilogue

LONDON—Spring.

Andrea Perkins had finished restoring a sixteenth century painting of a Venetian senator and was preparing to leave the Royal Academy of Arts when, at last, she understood the trick Michelangelo had played on them all. Suddenly she knew the truth about the portrait of David as surely as if the artist had written the painting's history with his own gifted hand. In a sense, he had.

She had looped the belt of her raincoat and was heading toward the front of the building that opened onto Trafalgar Square when she stopped to admire an engraving of *Leda* by Cornelis Bos. It depicted the Greek goddess Leda, the mother of the Gemini Twins, embracing their father, the god Zeus, who had taken the form of a swan.

Beneath the engraving was a brass plaque that informed the viewer that Cornelis Bos had been inspired by a drawing copied from a painting (now lost) by Michelangelo. Michelangelo's original painting was known only from copies by his students and descriptions from their journals. One of the copies hung next to the engraving and was signed by Sebastiano Luciani.

Andrea leaned the tote bag full of her equipment against the wall and studied Luciani's copy more carefully, thinking again of the portrait of David and the day she had learned that it was a fake.

Unlike Vittorio, she had begun to feel uneasy when the computer established the year as 1495. And though to the eye the signature looked exactly as Michelangelo Buonarroti would have signed his name, the computer was more discerning. The pressure the painter had applied to the brush was much greater than Michelangelo would have used, and the distance between the letters was wider.

There was no room for disagreement. A signature was as conclusive as a fingerprint. But the real contradiction about the portrait of David was: Why had the genuine Medici Medallion been affixed to a painting that bore a false signature?

In the months that followed the examination of the painting the priest had given Andrea, she had reread every account of Michelangelo's life, looking for clues. There was the frustration of the paradox, but there were lighter moments. It was amusing, while trying to track down a fifteenth century painting with a forged signature, to be reminded that Michelangelo was not above a little art forgery of his own.

As Tom Daley had been so delighted to point out to Vittorio Sassetti, early in the artist's career, Michelangelo had made fake Roman antiques and sent them to Rome to be sold. And in the days when Michelangelo studied with Ghirlandaio, he had fooled his teacher by substituting his own copies for ancient drawings by Masaccio. Using the trick of rubbing dirt into the pores of his sketch paper and darkening the edges with smoke from the fire in the hearth, the young genius had given his own sketches the appearance of age. His drawings were done so expertly that Ghirlandaio never discovered the deception.

When Andrea had exhausted the Michelangelo biographies, both authorized and unauthorized, and found no mention of the portrait of David, she began to investigate the Medici rulers of the period.

Piero, once established in Venice, began to make plans to recapture Florence. "The city will be greater than ever it was in the days of my father," he had written. He would prepare for his return, he added, by accumulating a collection of art, music, and literature that would equal if not surpass Lorenzo's, which had been confiscated and destroyed by Savonarola and his mob. One of his first moves toward that goal was to commission an easel painting by Michelangelo.

All this Andrea learned from an account in an obscure history of the Medici family. The account added that such a painting actually was delivered—though apparently it subsequently had been lost.

Not until today, in the Royal Academy of Art, had Andrea Perkins understood the contradiction of the genuine Medici Medallion on the portrait of David with the fake signature. But, having seen the reference on the Bos plaque to a lost painting by Michelangelo which was known only from copies by his students, she suddenly was sure she knew exactly what had happened to the Other David.

Piero de' Medici, she was sure, *had* received his easel painting of David. And this was indeed the same portrait the priest had given Andrea—the portrait now catalogued in the intra-city computer of Florence as "in the style of Michelangelo."

Whatever had inspired Michelangelo, spite . . . maliciousness . . . hatred of Piero . . . loyalty to Lorenzo . . . or a combination of these . . . the artist had accepted the commission and had painted a portrait of David but did not deliver it. Instead he allowed a protégé to copy it—to copy everything, including the signature. And then Michelangelo Buonarroti delivered the fake to Piero!

Andrea pulled the hood of her raincoat over her head and stepped through the impressive arch of London's Royal Academy into the soft afternoon rain. She cut through Trafalgar Square to Whitehall where she spotted and hailed a taxi. The cabbie jumped out, opened the back door and helped her in with a courteous bow. "Heathrow," she said, settling her tote bag beside her.

It seemed she spent half her time on airplanes now. When her year at the Accademia had ended, instead of continuing to work there as Vittorio Sassetti had urged her to, she had begun to free-lance as a restorer, and in the last few months had been to the Louvre in Paris, the Metropolitan in New York and the Royal Academy in London, along with the Accademia in Florence whenever Vittorio needed her help.

On the ride to the airport Andrea imagined the scene between Michelangelo and his protégé, probably Sebastiano Luciani, the same one who had made the copy of the *Leda*. She thought of Luciani as a fifteenth century Gino Corsini.

"An excellent copy, my dear Sebastiano," Michelangelo might have said.

"Ah, but my talent is only for copying. If I had your gift, maestro . . ."

"Today you will *be* Michelangelo." Buonarroti could not have resisted a chuckle. "Sign my name and I will deliver your copy to Piero de' Medici."

Then, Andrea thought, they must have had a big laugh and shared a bottle of wine, thinking of Piero stamping Sebastiano Luciani's copy with the precious mark of the Medici Medallion.

But what about Michelangelo's original portrait of David? What had become of it?

It would turn up sometime. It would be discovered in a trunk . . . or on the wall of an ancient villa . . . or

217

unidentified and forgotten in a vault at the Vatican. A year or two might pass, or ten, or two hundred, but the original portrait would reappear. She thought of Mark Twain's tribute, that "God created Italy from plans by Michelangelo." In that case, would the Creator not protect every last piece of the art of the Architect?

It was possible that Venice might, five hundred or a thousand years from now, slip permanently into the Adriatic. The Tower of Pisa might very well fall sometime over the next century. Leonardo's fresco of the Last Supper eventually could succumb to the blue fungus fostered by the moisture in Milan. And the ceiling of the Sistine Chapel with Michelangelo's *Story of Creation* might finally crash to the floor under its own weight.

But Andrea thought not. These masterpieces had endured. And they would endure. Someone in the future would find a way to preserve them. Surely that must have been covered in the Architect's contract.

A double-decker bus eased its way in front of Andrea's cab and claimed two-thirds of the narrow street for itself, slowing the cabbie's sprightly pace to a crawl.

Too bad, Andrea thought, that Michelangelo had not been able to make a provision in his plan for Italy to allot for himself the same number of years on earth as his art. It seemed unfair that the survival of his sculpture, architecture, and painting—even thus far—exceeded by so many years the puny number allotted the artist. But perhaps some small bargain had been struck. His eighty-nine years far, far surpassed the life span of most of his contemporaries. Time and Italy understood each other and made accommodations. Someone—sometime—would discover the missing portrait of David.

Suddenly excitement began to bubble up in Andrea as it had when she first realized that she might have discovered a painting by Michelangelo. The place to begin the search, she thought, would be to determine exactly who had been studying with Michelangelo in 1495. From there . . .

Andrea laughed silently to herself. How could she hope that she would be the one to find it? But how could she not hope?

"Can't you cut around the bus and go a little faster?" Andrea asked the cabbie, although she knew that arriving earlier would simply mean she would have to wait longer at the airport for her plane. There was no bargaining with time. And then she had an overwhelming awareness of how unfair it all was. What did a moment mean to a masterpiece? It had yesterday . . . it had tomorrow. But what of those who created art . . . who admired it . . . who placed a value on it . . . who stole it . . . killed or died for it?

"Time goes, you say?" She remembered the line from somewhere . . . "Ah, no, alas, Time stays, we go."

She dug into her tote bag for money to pay the cabbie. She wasn't really depressed. It must be the weather, she told herself. The bone-chilling dampness that was England's version of spring.

As she ran toward the terminal, her thoughts turned to the excitement she would feel when she arrived at Pisa Airport and Aldo Balzani stepped out of the waiting crowd to meet her. It would always be this way. Her heart would always stop for a moment when she saw him—or thought of him. She could not believe—rather, would not consider—that she and he would ever be anything but lithe and young and handsome. She was convinced that the truth they had found in each other would never alter as she measured the future by the Now . . . the only true gift Time ever gives.